Charge!

Ivanhoe and his exhausted horse were no match for Sir Brian's strong charge, and both horse and rider fell to the ground from the force of Sir Brian's lance. But, to everyone's surprise, Sir Brian also swayed in his saddle and fell, although Ivanhoe's lance had barely touched him.

Ivanhoe quickly rolled out from under his fallen horse. He drew his sword, ready to face Sir Brian....

READ ALL THE BOOKS
IN THE **wishbone** *classics* SERIES:

Wishbone Classics

IVANHOE

by Sir Walter Scott

retold by Joanne Mattern

Interior illustrations
by Ed Parker

Wishbone illustrations
by Kathryn Yingling

HarperPaperbacks

A Division of HarperCollinsPublishers

This is a work of fiction. The characters, incidents, and dialogues are products of the author's imagination and are not to be construed as real. Any resemblance to actual events or persons, living or dead, is entirely coincidental.

HarperPaperbacks *A Division of* HarperCollins*Publishers*
10 East 53rd Street, New York, N.Y. 10022

Copyright ©1997 Big Feats! Entertainment
All rights reserved. No part of this book may be used or reproduced in any manner whatsoever without written permission of the publisher, except in the case of brief quotations embodied in critical articles and reviews. For information address HarperCollins*Publishers*, 10 East 53rd Street, New York, N.Y. 10022.

Cover photographs by Carol Kaelson

A Creative Media Applications Production
Art Direction by Fabia Wargin Design

First printing: February 1997

Printed in the United States of America

HarperPaperbacks and colophon are trademarks of HarperCollins*Publishers*
WISHBONE is a trademark and service mark of Big Feats! Entertainment

❖ 10 9 8 7 6 5 4 3 2 1

Introduction

All set to enter a world of action, adventure, drama, and laughs? Then come along with me, **Wishbone**. You may have seen me on my TV show. Often I am the main character and sometimes I am the sidekick, but I'm always right in the middle of a thrilling story. Now, I'm going to be your guide as we explore one of the world's greatest books — IVANHOE. Together we'll meet a lot of interesting characters and discover places we've never been! I guarantee lots of surprises too! So find a nice comfy chair, and get ready to read with **Wishbone**.

Table of Contents

Sir Walter Scott created some of the most exciting novels ever written. The characters in Scott's novels faced many challenges as did Scott himself. His life was filled with many hardships. But just as his heroes overcame all odds, Scott truimphed over all the troubles in his life to become exactly what he wanted to be—a successful writer. Let's find out more about this extraordinary man.

Walter Scott was born in Edinburgh, Scotland, on August 15, 1771—about 600 years after the time of the story he tells in *Ivanhoe.*

Scott's family was well-known in Scotland. His grandfather had founded a famous medical school, and his ancestors had lived in the area for a long time. Households were often very large in those days, and the Scotts' was no exception: Walter was one of ten children!

When Scott was just a baby, he became very sick with an infection that left him unable to move for a time. He recovered, but his illness left him with a lifelong limp. However, his condition didn't stop Scott from finding adventure! He often spent hours walking across the moors, or fields, of his homeland. He also made good use of the time he spent in bed. From his family—especially his mother—Scott learned to love the poetry, legends, and history of his native land. Resting in bed, he had lots of time to read the Scottish legends he loved so much.

After he grew up, Scott studied law and got a job as a deputy sheriff. But his real love was writing. His first novel,

Waverley, was published in 1814. Scott published his work anonymously—his name was not on the book. The novel was so popular that Scott's later works were simply credited to "the author of *Waverley*."

Scott was a very busy guy! Along with writing books and working as a sheriff, he was also a partner in a publishing house. He loved to entertain guests at his huge estate, Abbotsford. There Scott lived like one of the rich men who were characters in his own novels. Scott also spent lots of time with his wife and their five children.

Scott was able to accomplish so much because he worked almost all day long. In fact, he barely slept and often did a full day's work before breakfast! In time, though, his busy schedule affected Scott's health. While he was writing *Ivanhoe*, he was so sick that he had to dictate, or tell, the story to one of his servants, who wrote it down for him.

Eventually, the public found out that Scott was the author of *Waverley* and the other novels, and he became the most famous author of his time. Scott was nicknamed "the Wizard of the North." In 1820, he was named a baronet, which is a title of British nobility. From that time on, he was known as Sir Walter Scott.

Scott's later years were difficult ones. His wife, Margaret, died, and his publishing house went bankrupt, leaving Scott with huge debts to pay. But Scott was not discouraged. He managed to pay off almost every penny he owed. He died in 1832, leaving behind a library full of novels of great adventure.

ABOUT IVANHOE

IVANHOE is set in England during the 1100s. Life was very different back then. A system called feudalism separated people into different classes. All the people were ruled by a king. A good king, such as King Richard, who appears in this book, could make life pleasant for all his subjects. But a bad king, like Richard's brother John could be a nightmare!

A king could not be everywhere at once. He needed help to run the country. So the king had the authority to give huge estates to noblemen called vassals. In return for property, vassals promised to obey the king, pay taxes and other fees to him, and join his army if the country should go to war.

Just as vassals served the king, serfs served the vassals. Serfs were the second lowest group in society. They worked for their lord, paid him rent, and basically did whatever he asked them to do. Serfs were also called peasants.

The serfs did not have much power, but at least they had their freedom. Slaves didn't even have that! Many vassals had slaves. Those men—and women—might be prisoners captured in battle or people who had no way of surviving except by selling themselves to a vassal. Slaves did all sorts of jobs. Some, like the characters Gurth and Wamba in *Ivanhoe*, were swineherds or entertainers. Others were maids or farm workers.

The dream of every nobleman was to become a knight. Young boys served in the homes of older knights, where they learned everything a knight needed to know. That learning usually did *not* include reading and writing.

Learning to ride a horse, use weapons like the sword and the lance, and fight in battle were more important.

Another important part of a knight's education was learning the code of chivalry. The code told a knight the proper way to behave. He was expected to be loyal to his king, respect women, be brave in battle, aid the helpless, and fight injustice. One of the most important rules of the code of chivalry was that a knight be true to his word. If a knight made a promise, he would keep it, no matter what.

A very special group of knights, called the Knights Templar, play a big part in this story. The Knights Templar were among the best fighters in the land. They had sworn a vow to defend the church, its properties, and its laws.

Many knights fought in the Crusades during the Middle Ages. Thousands undertook trips to the Holy Land (part of the Middle East, where Israel and the Arab countries are located today) to win back the city of Jerusalem from an enemy army. The journey was long and difficult, and the battles could be deadly. Many of the knights never came back.

At the time of *Ivanhoe*, England was made up of two distinct groups of people. The Saxons had lived in England for almost 1,000 years. But in 1066, a group of French soldiers called Normans (after Normandy, the part of France they were from) invaded England. Their leader, William the Conqueror, defeated the Saxons and became King of England. As you'll see in this story, the Saxons and the Normans were not on friendly terms! In fact, hundreds of years passed before the differences between the two groups were forgotten.

During this time, England was a dangerous place to live. Even the powerful knights weren't safe. Capturing anyone you could overpower was perfectly acceptable. Then, following the code of chivalry, you could demand that your prisoner pay a large ransom to win his or her freedom. Many desperate people lived in the woods, robbing and even killing. They made travel very dangerous and scary. Most people wouldn't set out on a journey without at least a few armed men to protect them. And no one—especially women—dared travel alone.

One last thing to keep in mind before we begin this thrilling tale of adventure is the attitude of the people in this book toward Jews. Two important characters in *Ivanhoe*, Isaac and his daughter Rebecca, are Jewish, and they are treated badly by many other characters in the book. Unfortunately, most people who lived in the Middle Ages did not like Jews. Because the Jews' culture and religion were different from what most people were used to, Jews were not trusted and were often hated. In this book, Sir Walter Scott was true to the attitudes of his time. Today, of course, we realize that such attitudes are wrong and that all people deserve respect.

MAIN CHARACTERS

The Saxons

Cedric — Ivanhoe's father and Rowena's guardian

Wilfred of Ivanhoe — Cedric's son, a loyal follower of King Richard

Rowena (roh WEE neh) — a 17-year-old girl, Cedric's ward

Athelstane (ATH el stayn) — a lord and Rowena's husband-to-be

Wamba — a jester or clown, Cedric's slave

Gurth — a swineherd, Cedric's slave

Locksley — leader of a group of outlaws

Friar Tuck — a priest and a member of Locksley's outlaws

The Normans

Richard the Lion-Hearted — the King of England

Prince John — Richard's younger brother; he acts as England's king while his brother is a prisoner in Austria

Prior Aymer (PRIGH er AY mer) — an important man of the church

Maurice de Bracy — a knight loyal to Prince John

Waldemar Fitzurse (VAWL deh mahr FITS erz) — a knight loyal to Prince John

Brian de Bois-Guilbert (deh BWAH-gil-bare) — a Knight Templar

Grand Master — ruler of the Knights Templar

Other

Isaac — a Jewish merchant from the city of York

Rebecca — Isaac's daughter

The Black Knight — a mysterious knight

SETTING

Important Places

Copmanhurst (COP man herst) — Friar Tuck's home in the woods

Rotherwood — Cedric's castle

Ashby de la Zouche (ASH bee deh lah ZEWSH) — location of the great tournament

Coningsburgh — Athelstane's castle

Torquilstone (TOR kill stohn) — castle where Cedric and his friends are held prisoners

Templestowe (TEM pel stoh) — home of the Knights Templar

1
Meeting in the Forest

Our story begins just as night is falling over a beautiful English forest. The scene is pretty, but unfortunately, things aren't as peaceful as they look. You see, England's King, Richard the Lion-Hearted, had been off on a Crusade. On his way home, King Richard was captured by an enemy in the country of Austria and thrown into a dungeon! In his absence his brother, Prince John, has seated himself on England's throne. Prince John is a cruel man who makes life very hard for his subjects. It's especially hard for Saxon serfs, like the two characters we're about to meet.

The sun was setting upon one of the rich, grassy fields of a large English forest. Here and there, the red rays of the sun shot through the leafy branches of the trees, lighting the paths that wound through the oaks and beeches. A small brook glided smoothly around a rock, its watery murmur the only sound in the hush of the forest.

Two human figures completed the landscape. The older one was wearing a simple jacket made of animal skin gathered close to his body by a broad leather belt. A horn and a two-edged knife were stuck through the belt. The man wore no hat, and his wild, thick hair hung around his face. It was clear from his clothes that he was a swineherd, in charge of pigs. The oddest thing about the man was a brass ring, like a dog's collar, fastened around his neck. It bore the inscription: "Gurth is the born thrall of Cedric of Rotherwood." **A thrall is a slave. The ring told everyone that Gurth is a slave belonging to a lord named Cedric. It's sort of like a big dog collar for humans.**

The second man sat on a rock beside his friend. He was some ten years younger than Gurth. Although he also wore a simple jacket, his had been dyed bright purple and decorated with colorful symbols and pictures. He also wore a red and yellow cloak, which he was fond of swirling about himself dramatically. On his head he wore a cap covered with silver bells that jingled loudly with every move he made and proclaimed him to be a jester or a clown. That man too wore the ring of a slave around his neck, proclaiming him to be "Wamba, the son of Witless, a thrall of Cedric of Rotherwood."

"A curse upon these infernal swine!" shouted Gurth. He blew his horn in an attempt to gather his pigs, which had scattered through the woods. But the animals were feasting on acorns or taking naps in the mud and paid no attention to him.

"A curse upon them and upon me too, if I do not get them home before dark!" Gurth cried. "Wamba, help me! Take a turn round the back of the hill and drive those animals before you."

"I could do that," Wamba said without moving. "But I have consulted my legs about this matter, and they are of the opinion that to carry me through the woods would be an unfriendly thing to do. Leave the pigs to their fate

"What—and have them eaten by some fat Norman?" Gurth exploded. "The Normans take everything from us. We already have little except the air we breathe, and that appears to be left to us only so we can endure the tasks the Normans lay upon our shoulders. The Normans get the finest and fattest animals for their food, while we unfortunate Saxons have nothing." **Gurth is complaining that the Saxons like himself do all the work, only to have the Normans take everything away from them. As far as Gurth can tell, the only reason the Saxons are allowed air to breathe is so that they can stay alive to work for the Normans. Gurth is obviously angry that the Normans have so much power and the Saxons have so little.**

"Gurth," said the jester, "I may be a fool, but even I know you should not say such things. If the Normans should ever hear that you have spoken against them, you are as good as dead."

"You would not betray me, would you?" Gurth asked.

"Betray you? No—that would be the trick of a wise man. I am a fool who has not the brains for such a deed. But wait! Hush! Whom have we here?" Wamba said suddenly, as the sound of horses came to their ears.

"Never mind them," answered Gurth, who had finally gotten his herd of pigs under control. "A terrible storm of thunder and lightning is raging just a few miles from us. You may be a fool, but credit me with some brains for once and let us go home before the storm begins!"

Wamba saw the sense in Gurth's suggestion, and the two set off. But Wamba was curious, and he kept turning around to catch a glimpse of the riders. He was soon rewarded, for the horsemen caught up with them on the road.

There were ten riders, but the two men in front were clearly the most important. One was Prior Aymer, an important man of the church. His chubby body was clothed in the finest of material, and his face bore a satisfied look, as if he was very happy with his life. He rode like a well-trained horseman, and silver bells decorated his mule's bridle. **In the Middle Ages, priests and other religious men were expected to live simply. Many of them used their position to get rich and weren't particularly holy at all! In his description of the Prior, Scott is telling us that the Prior is more concerned with looking elegant than with doing God's work.**

The other man was Sir Brian de Bois-Guilbert, a well-known member of the Knights Templar. He was strong, tall, and muscular. The stress of battle had stripped away any softness from his body, leaving nothing but bone and muscle. His face was deeply tanned and bore a savage expression, as if an angry storm might burst forth from him at any moment. He was dressed in full battle gear and rode a sturdy warhorse.

Wamba and Gurth bent their heads to show respect for the two important people. "God bless you, my children," the Prior said. "Can you show two of the humblest servants of the church where they might find food and a place to spend the night?"

"Two of the humblest servants of the church."

Wamba whispered to himself as he gazed at their fine clothes. "If they are humble, I should like to see their butlers and maids." Aloud, he said, "If you are looking for simple lodgings, you can follow that path to the home of the hermit of Copmanhurst. He is a religious man. I'm sure he would let you sleep under his roof." **A hermit is a person who lives alone and devotes his life to prayer. He lives simply—unlike the Prior and his friends!**

The Prior shook his head. "Churchmen do not like to impose on one another. We would rather give the common man a chance to serve God by serving us. No, we are looking for Rotherwood, the home of Cedric the Saxon."

"Most men would ask for shelter as a favor, but you are demanding it as your right," Gurth grumbled. "I don't know if I want to give directions to men with such an attitude."

"Don't argue with us, slave!" shouted Sir Brian. He spurred his war horse toward Gurth and raised the riding whip in his hand.

"Settle down, Sir Brian," the Prior said quickly. "There's no need to come to blows. My good fellow," he said to Wamba, "tell me the way to your master's house."

"I don't know if I can," Wamba complained. "Your companion has frightened the directions right out of my head." But finally he said, "You must stay on this road till you come to a sunken cross. Four paths meet there. If you take the path to the left, you will find the shelter you seek before the storm comes."

The Prior thanked Wamba, and the group rode on. As the sound of their hooves died away, Gurth said, "If

they follow your wise directions, they will hardly reach Rotherwood this night."

"I know," said Wamba with a grin. "I am not about to show the dog where the deer lies." **I like the way Wamba plays with words. What he really means is that he thinks the Prior and company might be dangerous to Cedric—the way a hunting dog is to a deer. That's why Wamba sends them in the wrong direction.**

Wamba and Gurth continued on with their herd of swine. Meanwhile, the travelers rode down the road in the direction Wamba had pointed them. Sir Brian said to the Prior, "What did those fellows mean by their rudeness? And why did you prevent me from punishing them for it?"

"One was just a fool, and the other is of that savage

race of Saxons who delight in showing their hatred for the Normans who conquered them," the Prior explained. "Beating those fellows would have only caused trouble between Cedric and ourselves. Remember what I told you about Cedric—he is a Saxon like his slave and as proud and fierce as anyone I've met."

The men soon reached the sunken cross and stopped to recall the directions Wamba had given them. "It is so dark, I can hardly see which road is which," the Prior complained. "He bid us turn to the left, I think."

"No, it was to the right," Sir Brian argued.

"The left!"

Each man insisted he was right, and so the group was at a standstill. Suddenly, Sir Brian noticed a man sleeping at the foot of the cross. One of the riders poked the sleeping figure, and the man jumped to his feet. He was a Palmer, wearing a cross made of palm leaves. **A Palmer is someone who has journeyed to the Holy Land.**

"I myself am headed to Rotherwood," the Palmer said when the Prior asked him for directions. "If I had a horse, I would be happy to guide you there, for the path is somewhat complicated."

The men agreed and allowed their guide to mount one of their horses. After a long journey through deep woods and soggy marshes, the group stood at last before the gates of Rotherwood, home of Cedric the Saxon. Sir Brian and the Prior were amazed that the Palmer had been able to find his way through such a complicated maze. Sir Brian blew his horn loudly to summon the gatekeeper just as the heavens opened and rain began to fall.

2
Dinner and a Challenge

Cedric is just sitting down to dinner when the Prior, Sir Brian, and their party arrive. Cedric is NOT in a very good mood, and the arrival of NORMAN guests doesn't do much to cheer him up.

Along oak table sat at the far end of the hall in Rotherwood, ready for Cedric the Saxon's evening meal. The floor of the room was made of dirt. At either end of the hall stood a huge fireplace, but as the chimneys were constructed in a very clumsy manner, at least as much of the smoke found its way into the hall as escaped from it. Over time, smoke had coated the rafters and beams of the ceiling with a thick, black layer of soot. Weapons and other implements of war hung on the walls.

Cedric's table sat on a step that raised it above the rest of the room. Massive oak chairs had been placed around the head table, where Cedric, his family, and any important visitors would sit. Other, smaller tables were meant for lesser visitors and the family's servants were offered only plain benches for seating.

Cedric sat alone at the head table, grumbling to himself. He was not very tall but broad-shouldered and powerfully built. His red face bore its usual expression of anger and displeasure. Cedric's ancestors were Saxon royalty, and he has spent his life defending his rights against those who would take them from him. He was always quick to jump into a fight if he felt his rights were in danger. His blond hair hung to his shoulders and showed little signs of gray, even though Cedric was approaching his 60th year.

"Where is the Lady Rowena?" Cedric snapped impatiently to Rowena's maid, who was standing behind the table. Cedric is Rowena's guardian who is a descendant of Saxon royal blood.

"She is changing her clothes," the servant replied. "Surely you would not want her to sit down to dinner in her muddy travel clothes!"

"Hmmph!" Cedric snorted. "And what keeps Gurth so long afield? I suppose something has happened to his herd." Cedric panicked and assumed the worst. "My faithful servant has been murdered and my goods taken and Wamba—where is Wamba? Did someone say he had gone forth with Gurth?"

Another servant nodded.

"Oh, this is even better!" Cedric yelled. "Next I shall hear that my Saxon fool has been carried off to serve a Norman lord. If that be true, I will be avenged!" He grabbed the spear that was always at his side. "My enemies think me old, but they shall find the blood of heroes in my veins, even though I am alone. Ah, Wilfred, my son," he said in a quieter voice. "If only you could have controlled your passions. I would not have disinherited you, and I would not be left here alone like an oak in a storm." Recalling Wilfred, his lost son, seemed to take the fire out of Cedric. He sat down and put his head in his hands. **To disinherit someone means to declare they are no longer part of your family. Cedric disinherited**

Wilfred of Ivanhoe because his son disobeyed him by going to fight for King Richard in the Crusades—and because he was angry that Ivanhoe was in love with Cedric's ward, Rowena.

The blast of a horn shattered Cedric's gloomy thoughts. The gatekeeper hurried in and announced, "The Prior and the knight Brian de Bois-Guilbert request food and lodging for the night for themselves and their servants. They are on their way to the tournament at Ashby de la Zouche."

"Norman guests!" Cedric exclaimed in disgust. "I would rather leave them outside, but Norman or Saxon, the hospitality of Rotherwood cannot be denied, especially in these dangerous times. Let them in." **Here's another example of chivalry. Even though Cedric doesn't like Normans and doesn't want them in his home, he is bound to honor any request for shelter.** He turned to Rowena's maid. "You may tell Rowena that she does not have to dine with us if she doesn't want to."

"I am sure she will want to," the maid replied. "Sir Brian has lately returned from the Holy Land, and you know Lady Rowena is always eager for news from there."

"The Holy Land!" Cedric spat. "I too might be interested in such talk if my son had not disobeyed me and gone to fight there with King Richard. But I care no more for his fate than that of the most worthless pilgrim in the land!"

Cedric's outburst was interrupted by the arrival of the guests in the dining hall. The Prior and Sir Brian took seats at the head table, while their servants settled at the tables farther down the room. The Palmer who had guided the men to Rotherwood slipped unnoticed into a spot by the fireplace.

Just as the feast was about to begin, a door opened beside the table and a servant announced, "The Lady Rowena!" Then Rowena, accompanied by her maids, stepped into the room. All stood up to greet her as she took her place beside Cedric.

All the men present could not take their eyes off Rowena. She was the most beautiful girl they had ever seen. She was tall and fair, with beautiful skin. Her thick blond hair was arranged in cascading ringlets braided with sparkling gems, and her blue eyes were warm enough to melt any man's heart.

Rowena soon noticed several of the men staring at her. Their attention embarrassed her. She quickly drew her veil around her face, hoping the knights would realize how uncomfortable she was.

Talk soon turned to the upcoming tournament at Ashby. **A tournament was a huge sporting event. Knights battled one another in a number of different contests, and great crowds gathered to see who would be the champion.** "I hope you and the Lady Rowena will travel with us to Ashby," the Prior said. "We are sure to be safe from all bandits with brave Sir Brian to escort us."

"No, I have always relied on my own sword and my faithful followers to protect me. I will not rely on any Norman knights," Cedric said proudly. "We intend to travel to Ashby with my neighbor and friend, Athelstane of Coningsburgh, descendant of the last Saxon monarchs of England." **The roads were filled with bandits and other dangers in the Middle Ages, so it was smart to travel armed and in a large group, even with a small army, just to be safe!**

Just then, a servant came to tell Cedric that another traveler was at the gate, seeking shelter from the storm. "He is a Jew who calls himself Isaac of York," the servant whispered. "Shall I let him in?"

"A Jew!" exclaimed Sir Brian. The Prior seemed equally upset at the thought of having a Jew in their presence.

"Peace," Cedric said. "I will deny my hospitality to no one, not even a Jew. He may enter, but I will not force anyone here to sit with him."

A tall, thin, old man shuffled into the room. Black eyes peered out from a weathered face, half-hidden by the man's long, gray hair and beard. He was wrapped in a plain-colored cloak and wore the odd-looking yellow square cap that all Jews were required to wear. He swept the cap from his head in a gesture of humility and respect and greeted Cedric warmly. But the master of the house simply nodded coldly and gestured for Isaac to take a place at the far end of the room.

No one seated at the lower tables would make room for Isaac. The poor man stood looking around for a friendly face or a welcoming glance. **Why this attitude? Jews were hated during the Middle Ages because they were different. People didn't understand them, and they didn't trust them either. In fact, Jews were often blamed for anything that went wrong. They were unfairly made scapegoats for other people's problems.**

Finally the Palmer stood up from his place by the

fire. "Here, old man," the Palmer said. "My clothes have dried and I have eaten my fill, but you are wet and hungry." He settled Isaac into his spot near the fire and brought him some food to eat. Before the old man could thank him, the Palmer moved to a spot near the head table so he could join in the conversation there.

Sir Brian, the Prior, and Cedric were engaged in a lively discussion about the knights who had gone on Crusade. Sir Brian had commanded the Knights Templar when he was in the Holy Land. He was the bravest of all the knights and feared nothing. Talking of war was one of his favorite things, and he named many Norman knights who had shown bravery in battle. Their conversation distressed Rowena, and she said, "Were there no Saxons whose names are worthy to be mentioned?"

"Forgive me, my lady," said Sir Brian. "King Richard did indeed take a host of brave Saxon warriors to the Holy Land."

"Indeed," said the Palmer in a firm, strong voice. "The English of Saxon blood who fought in the Holy Land were second to none. I saw King Richard himself and five Saxon knights at a tournament where they defeated even the Knights Templar. Sir Brian knows what I am talking about."

The Saxons beat the best of the best!

Sir Brian's face darkened with bitter rage at the memory of losing a tournament, and his fingers gripped the hilt of his sword.

It was all he could do not to attack the Palmer for what he had said.

Cedric, meanwhile, was so happy to hear that Saxon knights had fought bravely, he didn't even notice Sir Brian's rage. "I will give you a golden bracelet if you tell me the names of those six knights who upheld England's honor," he said.

"I will gladly tell you," said the Palmer. "But you may keep your golden bracelet. The first knight was King Richard the Lion-Hearted." He went on to name four knights of noble birth and Saxon blood.

"And the sixth man?" Cedric said eagerly.

The Palmer was silent for a long moment before he answered. At last he said, "The sixth was a young knight of lower rank. I don't remember his name."

"I cannot believe you have forgotten," said Sir Brian scornfully. "I myself will tell the name of the knight who defeated me at the tournament. It was the Knight of Ivanhoe. Yet I say that were he in England and dared repeat his challenge at the tournament at Ashby, I would be happy to fight him again."

"Your challenge will soon be answered," the Palmer vowed. "I myself will swear that he will meet you as soon as he returns to England."

"I too swear that Ivanhoe will meet every challenge," Rowena said boldly.

Cedric had been silent through that part of the conversation. Pride, resentment, and embarrassment chased one another across his broad face like shadows drifting over a field as he thought of Ivanhoe, his disinherited son.

The hour grew late, and Sir Brian and the Prior headed off to bed. The Palmer also left for the room where he would sleep that night. But he didn't get far before one of Lady Rowena's maids came to tell him he was wanted in the lady's chamber.

What could Lady Rowena possibly want to discuss secretly with the Palmer? Might it be something to do with Ivanhoe?

3
A Secret Departure

The Palmer entered Lady Rowena's room and found her seated with her maids. At the sight of her visitor, Rowena dismissed her servants so she could talk with the Palmer privately.

"Pilgrim," Rowena said nervously, "tonight Sir Brian mentioned a name—the name Ivanhoe. I ask you now, where is he? Was he all right when you saw him last?" **Rowena is in love with Ivanhoe. But Cedric has plans to wed Rowena to Athelstane. Cedric's dream is that England will once again be ruled by Saxons of royal blood and that Athelstane and Rowena will sit on the throne. Is it just me, or were the Middle Ages complicated?**

"I know little of the Knight of Ivanhoe," the Palmer replied, keeping his cloak wrapped tightly around his face. "I wish I could tell you more, since you are so interested in his fate. I believe he will return to England any day now. You would know better than I what his chance at happiness is here."

The Lady Rowena sighed deeply. "Is there nothing else you can tell me about him? How did Ivanhoe look when you saw him last? Was he sick?" she added, her face filled with worry.

"He was darker and thinner than when he first arrived, and he seemed very concerned about something."

"He will find little here to cheer him," Rowena said.

"When you mentioned Ivanhoe's name in the hall tonight, many of the people there should have been glad to hear it. But I am the only one who dares to ask you anything about him," Rowena added sadly. "If only Ivanhoe were here now and able to fight in the upcoming tournament! I fear that if Athelstane of Coningsburgh wins the tournament, Cedric will give him my hand in marriage. Those will surely be evil tidings for Ivanhoe." She sighed again. "I thank you, good pilgrim, for telling me about my friend. I will keep you no longer."

The Palmer left Rowena's chamber and headed to a far corner of the building. Here the rooms were not as elegant as Lady Rowena's, for they were mostly meant for servants. "Does Isaac the Jew sleep in one of these rooms?" he asked a passing servant. The man pointed out one of the smallest, shabbiest rooms. "And where is the swineherd, Gurth?" the Palmer asked. "Has he returned to the castle?" The Palmer nodded at the servant's answer, then entered his own room and settled down to sleep. **Why is the Palmer so curious about where certain people are sleeping? I think he's up to something!**

The Palmer woke as the earliest sunbeams were peeking through the grated window of his chamber. He dressed and hurried to Isaac's room.

The old man was sleeping restlessly, as if struggling with nightmares. He jumped, startled, when the Palmer shook him awake, and stared at him in wild surprise.

"Fear nothing from me, Isaac," said the Palmer. "I come as your friend. If you do not leave this house instantly and travel quickly, your journey may prove to be very dangerous! I overheard Sir Brian talking to his servants in the hall last night. He told them to watch you carefully and rob you as soon as you were some distance from Rotherwood."

The terror that seized Isaac at the Palmer's words is impossible to describe. Isaac's head dropped to his chest, and his knees buckled until he fell to the floor at the Palmer's feet. "Holy God of Abraham, protect me!" he cried.

"Stand up," the Palmer said impatiently. "I will tell you how to escape. Leave now, while everyone is still asleep. I will guide you by the secret paths of the forest, and I will not leave you until you are safe. Follow me."

The Palmer led the way to the chamber where Gurth was sleeping. "Wake up," he said. "Wake up and undo the gate for Isaac and me."

Gurth was rather annoyed at the commanding tone of the Palmer's voice. He did not move from his bed. "Both of you will have to wait until the opening of the front gate," he said. "We allow no visitors to sneak away so early." Wamba the Fool, who had entered the room behind the Palmer, nodded his agreement. **In the old days, the gates of a castle were locked at night to keep bandits and other bad guys from sneaking in while everyone was asleep.**

"Nevertheless," said the Palmer, "you will not refuse me this favor." So saying, he leaned down and whispered something in Gurth's ear. Gurth jumped up as if electrified and hurried to do as the Palmer had asked.

"What about my mule?" Isaac asked as they stood outside.

"Fetch him his mule," the Palmer said to Gurth, "and fetch one for me as well. I will return it to Cedric at Ashby."

"Most willingly shall it be done," Gurth said and ran toward the stables.

"I wish I knew what you Palmers learn in the Holy Land," Wamba said in surprise. "I can't imagine what you said to make Gurth follow your commands." The Palmer only smiled.

Gurth soon returned with the mules, and Isaac and the Palmer hurried into the forest. The Palmer led the way down secret, twisted paths until they were far from any danger of pursuit.

"I cannot thank you enough for your kindness and protection," Isaac said. "I don't know how to repay you."

"I desire no reward," the Palmer said.

"Wait!" Isaac insisted. "I can give you what you need most. You need a horse and armor, don't you?"

The Palmer turned in surprise. "How did you know?"

"I can tell from the way you talk that you are a knight," said Isaac, "and I saw the glint of gold spurs under your jacket. **A man received a set of gold spurs when he was knighted. They were a sign of his new rank.** Surely you will be taking part in the tournament along with all the other knights. If a horse and armor are what you need, I can supply them." With that, he wrote a letter on a piece of paper and gave it to the Palmer. "Go to the city and present this letter to my friend. He will give you your choice of horses and armor, and you can return them to him after the tournament. I suggest that you choose the armor inlaid with gold and the gallant black horse."

"But what if I lose the armor in the tournament?" the Palmer asked. "You know that if a knight is defeated, he must give his armor and his horse to the victor."

Isaac looked surprised at the possibility. "No, it is impossible for that to happen to a brave knight such as yourself," he said. "Fare thee well, good youth! And be careful—not just for the sake of the horse and the armor but for your own life and limbs as well." With that, the two men parted, each riding his separate way.

4
The Disinherited Knight

King Richard is the rightful ruler of England, but as we mentioned, he's stuck in a dungeon far away in Austria. Who is running the country while he's gone? Richard's little brother, Prince John. Now Prince John is a pretty rotten guy, and he hates the Saxons, who make up much of England's population. Instead of taking care of England's people, he's stealing from them! And rather than worrying about his brother Richard, John and his friends hope he NEVER comes home! Let's join the action at Ashby de la Zouche.

No one wanted to miss the excitement of a great tournament. The morning of the tournament found huge crowds gathering on the field at Ashby. Cedric the Saxon and his ward, Rowena, were among the spectators and so was Cedric's friend Athelstane. Even Isaac, the old Jewish man who had been saved by the Palmer, was there, accompanied by his beautiful daughter, Rebecca. Her brilliant eyes and pearly white teeth gave her a beauty equaling that of any woman at the tournament. Long, thick curls of dark hair tumbled from a turban of yellow silk decorated with a large ostrich feather, and her flowered silk dress was set off by a priceless diamond necklace.

The lists were surrounded by a strong wooden fence. **The "lists" was the name for the fields where a tournament took place.** The fighters entered the lists through openings at the northern and southern ends of the fence. A herald stood before each opening to announce the name and rank of a knight as he entered. Outside the fence surrounding the lists were five colorful tents belonging to the best of all the knights. And everywhere were the spectators, sitting on the benches of the wooden galleries or even on the grass itself, peering eagerly toward the ground where the action was about to take place.

One gallery was raised higher than the ground around it and held a throne. Prince John would sit there. Opposite that gallery was another one, gaily decorated. It contained another throne, surrounded by beautiful young maidens. The throne bore an inscription stating it was reserved for the Queen of Beauty and Love. But no one knew who would have the honor of sitting there.

A blast of trumpets announced the entrance of Prince John and his men. He was seated on an elegant horse. The Prince was splendidly dressed in crimson and gold, and his head was covered by a rich fur hat decorated with precious stones. Long, wavy hair flowed over his shoulders. He cackled with pleasure at the sight of all his people and rejoiced in the power he held. Beside him rode his chief advisers, Waldemar Fitzurse and Maurice De Bracy. Both men were strong and tall, mighty knights who had seen many battles.

When Prince John saw the empty throne awaiting

the Queen of Beauty and Love, he said to his men, "We have neglected to name our fair queen for today. I care not who wins the honor."

"Why don't we let the champion of the lists name the Queen of Beauty and Love," De Bracy suggested. "It will add another honor to his triumph and teach fair ladies to prize the love of valiant knights."

Prince John agreed. He settled onto his own throne, and the tournament finally began.

One of the heralds announced that Prince John had selected the five best Norman knights as champions for the tournament. They would fight anyone who challenged them. If the challenger touched a champion's shield with the flat end of his lance, it indicated his desire to fight with boards fastened to the tips of their lances, so no one would get hurt. But if he touched the shield with the point of his lance, the two would fight with sharp weapons. **A lance is a long, sharp spear used by men on horseback. If the knights fight with uncovered lances they risk being killed!**

The five champions rode forward onto the lists. Among them were Sir Brian and other members of the Knights Templar. All were splendidly armed and mounted on large, high-spirited warhorses. Plenty of other knights, both Norman and Saxon, were eager to challenge the champions, although all chose to fight with their lances covered, for safety.

Battle was soon joined, and the crowd cheered at the exciting sight before them. Each champion rode forward at full speed to meet his challenger. When they met in the middle of the lists, each knight struck at the other with his lance, trying to throw the other man from his horse. There was a tremendous noise as lances and shields crashed against one another. The force of the blows sent many knights tumbling to the ground.

It soon became clear that the Knights Templar were getting the best of their opponents. Cedric and Rowena leaned forward eagerly, not wanting to miss a single moment of the action. No one was more dissatisfied that the Saxon knights were losing the contest than Cedric. Alas, he was not trained in warfare, so he could not challenge any of the Norman champions. But perhaps Athelstane would.

"The day is against the Saxons, my lord," Cedric said to Athelstane. "Are you not tempted to take the field?"

But Athelstane, though strong of heart and body, did not want to join the battle. "I will fight in the general battle tomorrow," he said lazily. "It isn't worth it for me to tire myself out today." He gnawed on a fat chicken leg he was holding. "Anyway, I hate to fight on a full stomach," he mumbled.

Cedric was disappointed. Athelstane was the last of the Saxon royal house, and Cedric dreamed of the day when his friend would resume his rightful place on England's throne. But although Athelstane was stout of heart and powerful of body, he was not eager to exert himself by fighting. Cedric couldn't understand how a man with royal Saxon blood flowing through his veins could be so lazy.

As the battle went on, it became obvious that Sir Brian was the best fighter in the lists. Prince John was ready to award the prize to him, when suddenly a solitary trumpet note cut through the air. All eyes turned to see a new challenger ride onto the field.

This knight was slender and graceful. He wore a fine suit of armor, inlaid with gold. His shield bore a picture of a young oak tree pulled up by the roots, with the word *Disinherited* written underneath. He trotted his gallant black horse past Prince John and the spectators and saluted the ladies so gracefully that they immediately began to cheer him. **No one can see the knight's face because the visor, or front, of his helmet is closed. But I know it's the Palmer who was at Cedric's house. Remember how he helped Isaac escape and how Isaac thanked him by arranging for the loan of a fine suit of armor and a horse?**

Without pausing, the Disinherited Knight rode straight up to Sir Brian and touched the sharp end of his spear to the Knight Templar's shield.

> Wow! The Disinherited Knight has just challenged the champion to a fight to the death!

"Are you so eager to see the face of God?" Sir Brian asked. "You are putting your life in great danger."

"I am fitter to meet God than you are," answered the Disinherited Knight.

"Then take your place on the lists and prepare to look your last upon the sun," Sir Brian said. **Sir Brian sure is confident that he's going to win.**

The two knights rode their horses to the far ends of the lists. The crowd leaned forward eagerly. Few believed that the Disinherited Knight could triumph, yet they all hoped he would somehow be victorious.

The trumpets sounded and the two knights thundered forward. They crashed together in the center of the lists with the shock of a thunderbolt, and their lances burst into slivers, but each managed to stay on his horse.

The two opposing knights glared at each other with eyes that seemed to flash fire through the bars of their visors. Then each rode his horse back to the far ends of the lists and received a fresh lance for the next pass.

In the second encounter, Sir Brian hit the center of the Disinherited Knight's shield so hard that the young knight reeled in his saddle. But the Disinherited Knight struck a blow of his own, lodging the point of his lance in the visor of Sir Brian's helmet. The shock ripped the saddle from the horse's back and sent saddle, horse, and man tumbling to the ground.

Sir Brian got quickly to his feet. Angrier than ever at being unhorsed, he drew his sword and waved it threateningly at his foe. The Disinherited Knight jumped from his horse, drawing his sword too. But before they could come to blows, the marshals rode between them and reminded them that the laws of the tournament did not allow them to fight with swords.

"We will meet again," Sir Brian snarled, "and then there will be no one to separate us."

"On foot or on horseback, with spear, with ax, or with sword, I am ready to fight you," the Disinherited Knight replied. As Sir Brian angrily rode away, the

Disinherited Knight called out, "Here's to all true English hearts!" Then he challenged the other four champions to fight him.

The four battles that followed did not last long. The Disinherited Knight made short work of all four Norman knights and was declared the winner of the day.

When the Disinherited Knight stepped before Prince John to receive his prize, he refused to raise his visor and reveal his identity. Prince John was not happy that all his chosen champions had been defeated. He said to his marshals, "This knight must have been disinherited of his courtesy as well as his family, since he appears before me without uncovering his face. Does anyone know who he is?"

"I cannot guess," answered De Bracy.

"All I can think is that he is one of the fine soldiers who accompanied King Richard to the Holy Land," ventured Fitzurse.

"Perhaps it is King Richard himself," said a voice in the crowd.

The Prince's face turned as pale as death. "God forbid!" he swore.

"Don't worry, Your Grace," said Fitzurse. "Your brother is a much bigger man than this suit of armor could ever hold."

The marshals escorted the Disinherited Knight forward. Prince John was still shaken by the thought that his brother, whom he had betrayed, might be standing before him. But he pushed that disturbing thought from his mind as best he could and told the knight, "Your bravery and strength this day has won you a fine warhorse. It is also your duty and privilege to name the lady who will preside over tomorrow's festivities as the Queen of Beauty and Love. Raise your lance."

The knight obeyed, and Prince John placed a delicate gold crown lined with green satin on its point. Prince John expected him to crown one of the ladies sitting in the royal box, for they were the Prince's chosen favorites. But the Disinherited Knight carried his prize past all the ladies seated near the Prince and presented it to the fair Lady Rowena.

"Long live Lady Rowena!" the crowd shouted as the golden crown was placed on her head. "Long live the Queen of Beauty and Love!"

So ended the first day of the tournament.

Now THIS is my idea of adventure! An unknown knight comes out of nowhere to defeat all of Prince John's champions. And he crowns Rowena as his queen of the day. But the tournament isn't over, and more excitement is just around the corner!

5
An Identity Revealed

It's day two of the tournament. Our friend the Palmer who we now know as the Disinherited Knight, is preparing to take the field. Today's contest is to be a melee, a pretend war between two teams of knights. Here we go!

Morning dawned in unclouded splendor. The sun was barely above the horizon when a crowd began to gather at the lists. Everyone wanted to find a good seat from which to watch the upcoming battle.

Soon the marshals and heralds appeared on the field to announce who would make up the two armies that were to fight that day. Because the Disinherited Knight had triumphed over all other knights the day before, he would command one side. Sir Brian was ranked as the previous day's second best, so he was named commander of the other army. The two groups of knights would fight until Prince John signaled an end to the battle.

About ten o'clock, Prince John and his men arrived, announced by a great fanfare of trumpets. About the same time, Cedric the Saxon and his ward, Rowena, took their places in the gallery. Cedric's friend Athelstane, however, was not with them, as he was going to fight in the upcoming battle. Much to Cedric's surprise and dismay, Athelstane had chosen to fight on the side of the Norman Sir Brian and the Knights Templar. Cedric argued strongly about Athelstane's rightful place, but Athelstane was too stubborn to change his mind.

Athelstane had not told Cedric, but he was jealous of the attention the Disinherited Knight had paid to Rowena. It had long been understood between Cedric and Athelstane that Athelstane would someday marry Rowena. When the Disinherited Knight chose Rowena as Queen of Beauty and Love, Athelstane became determined to fight his rival and put him in his proper place.

Most of the best knights were fighting on Sir Brian's side, at Prince John's special request. He had no intention of having Sir Brian, one of his favorite knights, meet defeat again at the hands of the Disinherited Knight.

Prince John settled Rowena in her seat of honor as Queen of Beauty and Love, and a burst of music announced that the battle was to begin. The knights spurred their horses into a full gallop and met with a deafening crash in the center of the field. Lances cracked against shields, and both horses and men roared with excitement. The smell of blood filled the air.

Amid huge clouds of dust, the knights battled back and forth across the field. First the advantage was with one side; then it shifted to the other. Knights fell screaming from their horses, their armor covered with dust and blood, while the crowd shouted encouragement.

Knights who had fallen from their horses but were still able to fight rushed forward, waving their swords.

Small hand-to-hand battles began to spring up all over the field. No holds were barred in the fighting; only death, serious injury, or capture would cause a knight to give up the battle.

After a time, only the best fighters were left on the field. It soon became clear that the Disinherited Knight was in trouble. Athelstane attacked him from one side, while Sir Brian attacked from the other, trapping the Disinherited Knight in the middle. Only the young knight's horsemanship kept him mounted and safe. He turned his horse around and around, dealing sweeping blows with his sword. But horse and man were tiring, and the Disinherited Knight seemed to have no way of escaping defeat.

"Why don't you signal an end to the fight?" Fitzurse asked Prince John. "The Disinherited Knight is in serious trouble."

"If he is as good a fighter as everyone thinks he is, let us see if he can get out of his trouble," Prince John replied. He did not like the mysterious knight, and he was looking forward to seeing him soundly defeated—or even killed.

Among the Disinherited Knight's army rode a knight in black armor, mounted on a black horse. All at once, the Black Knight spurred his horse forward, shouting "To the rescue!" He rode straight at Athelstane and wrenched the battle ax right out of the Saxon's hand. Then he dealt such a powerful blow that Athelstane tumbled from his horse and lay senseless on the field. The Black Knight's presence evened the odds against the Disinherited Knight. Seeing that his leader could now turn his attention completely to Sir Brian, the Black Knight rode away from the main conflict.

Sir Brian's horse had been wounded, and he was no match for the Disinherited Knight. The horse fell, and Sir Brian rolled onto the field. But his foot was stuck in the horse's stirrup, and he could not jump to his feet as the Disinherited Knight approached him. Waving his sword over his fallen foe, the Disinherited Knight commanded him to give up. Before Sir Brian could be injured or killed, Prince John signaled an end to the contest. The Disinherited Knight was the clear winner.

Now that the battle was over, the audience could see the field clearly. It was littered with the broken bodies of fallen knights. Squires ran forward to help their masters, leading those who could still walk off the field. The more seriously injured were carried away on stretchers.

It was time for Prince John to name the knight who had done best that day. To everyone's surprise, he called for the Black Knight to be brought forward.

"Your Grace, the Disinherited Knight won the battle," the Prince's men pointed out to him. "He single-handedly defeated six champions and unhorsed Sir Brian."

"The Disinherited Knight would have lost had the Black Knight not come to his aid," Prince John insisted, for he did not want to acknowledge the man who had beaten the Norman champion, Sir Brian. "We will award the prize to the Black Knight."

To everyone's surprise, however, the Black Knight could not be found. He had left the lists at the battle's end and had ridden into the forest. Another winner would have to be named. Prince John now had no excuse to deny the honor to the Disinherited Knight.

The Disinherited Knight was led forward through a field slippery with blood and cluttered with broken armor and dead and wounded horses. "Disinherited Knight," Prince John announced, "for the second time we award you the honors of this tournament. You have the right to claim and receive from the hands of the Queen of Beauty and Love the crown of honor that your bravery justly deserves."

While the trumpets sounded and the crowd cheered, the marshals brought the Disinherited Knight to Rowena's throne. The Disinherited Knight knelt at her feet, and the beautiful Rowena leaned forward to crown him.

"Wait!" the marshals cried suddenly. "His head must be bare." The Disinherited Knight tried to stop them, but it was no use. The marshals pulled off his helmet, revealing a young man, about 25 years old, with a sunburned nose and short blond hair. His face was as pale as death and marked with streaks of blood.

Rowena had no sooner seen the knight's face than she let out a faint shriek. She knew this man—he was her beloved, Sir Wilfred of Ivanhoe! Her hands trembling with emotion, she placed the crown on the knight's head and proclaimed, "I bestow on you this crown, Sir Knight, as a reward for today's bravery." Then she paused and added, "And never was a man more worthy of this honor!" Her eyes shone with love as she gazed down at the man she had feared was gone from her life forever.

The knight bent his head and kissed Rowena's hand. Then he fell forward and fainted at her feet.

Cedric, who had been stunned at the sudden appearance of his banished son, now rushed forward as if to separate him from Rowena. But the marshals had already done that. The men undid Ivanhoe's armor and found the reason he had fainted. The point of a lance had penetrated his armor and caused a terrible wound in his side.

Oh, no! Ivanhoe has returned in triumph, but now he's been badly wounded! Will he recover from his injury and be able to marry his beloved Rowena?

6
A Show of Skill

As the marshals took the injured Ivanhoe away, news of the Disinherited Knight's true identity reached the ears of Prince John. When he found out that the man who had defeated Sir Brian had fought with King Richard in the Holy Land, the Prince hated the knight more than ever.

"Clearly, the Queen of Beauty and Love cares a great deal for Ivanhoe," the Prince commented to De Bracy and Fitzurse as they relaxed in the Prince's tent. "All could see her grief when she realized Ivanhoe was injured. Who is this Lady Rowena?"

"She is a Saxon heiress of great property," replied one of his men, "a rose of loveliness and a jewel of wealth."

An heiress is someone who will inherit a large amount of money.

"Really?" Prince John said with interest. "Then let us cheer her sorrows by wedding her to a fine Norman knight instead of the wounded Saxon, Ivanhoe. What do you say, De Bracy? Would you like to gain fair lands by wedding a Saxon maiden?"

Wait a minute! Doesn't Rowena get any say about whom she's going to marry? Actually, no. In the Middle Ages, people usually married for

money, not for love. A young woman's guardians—or even a king or a prince—decided whom she should marry. The wishes of a king or a prince were granted over all others. You can bet that a woman who had a lot of money or property, as Rowena does, had lots of fellows interested in her!

De Bracy eagerly agreed, and the matter was settled. Before Prince John could inform Cedric and Rowena of his decision to marry Rowena to De Bracy, a messenger delivered a sealed letter to the Prince. Prince John read the few words there and turned pale. He pulled De Bracy aside and whispered, "This message says that my brother Richard has regained his freedom from his captors in Austria!"

"Perhaps it is a false alarm," De Bracy said, trying not to worry at the terrible news.

"No, this messenger is completely trustworthy. We must end the tournament and prepare for Richard's return to England." **Why is John so nervous at the news that his brother is no longer a prisoner in Austria? Because, Prince John is not ruling England the way King Richard wanted him to. The Prince and his friends know that Richard is going to be very angry with them when he returns to England and finds out what's been going on!**

"The crowd will be upset if the tournament ends so soon," De Bracy said. "They are eager to see tomorrow's archery contest."

"It is still early," said Fitzurse. "Let us have the archers compete today. That way, we can end the tournament early and still satisfy the crowd."

Prince John agreed. An announcement was made to the crowd, explaining that John's princely duties called him away early and a change in plans was necessary. The archery contest scheduled for tomorrow would take place right away.

At the end of the preliminary competitions, the eight finest archers in the land remained. Prince John was pleased to see that several of them were men in his service. However, one Saxon stranger dressed in green struck Prince John as a bold fellow.

"Are you going to try for the prize?" Prince John asked him.

"I don't think I should," the man replied. "I don't know how Your Grace will feel when I defeat your own men."

Prince John flushed with rage. "What is your name?" he demanded.

Hmm, Locksley...dressed all in green...good with a bow and arrow...

"Locksley," the man replied.

"Well, Locksley, since you are so sure of yourself, you will shoot against the best of these archers."

"What if I don't care to do that?" Locksley asked boldly.

"Then I shall have my marshals cut your bowstring, break your bow and arrows, and drive you from the field as a coward!" Prince John snarled.

Upon hearing that, Locksley agreed to the Prince's terms. Still, Prince John told his men, "Watch this man Locksley closely, lest he try to escape. I don't trust him."

One by one, the archers stepped forward into the lists and loosed their arrows at the target. Hubert, a man loyal to Prince John, was the only man to lodge two arrows within the inner ring of the target. As the best archer, he prepared to face Locksley.

A fresh target was brought out. Hubert shot first. He took careful aim, measuring the distance with his eye while he tested the tension of his bow. At last he stretched the bowstring all the way back to his ear and let his arrow fly. The arrow whistled through the air and landed within the inner ring of the target but not exactly in the center.

"You did not allow for the wind, Hubert," Locksley said, "or that would have been a better shot." As he spoke, he stepped forward and took his shot so carelessly, it seemed he had not even looked at the target. Yet the arrow landed two inches nearer to the center than Hubert's had.

"If you let this rude fellow beat you, you deserve to be hanged!" Prince John snarled angrily at Hubert.

"A man can but do his best," Hubert replied calmly. Calculating the effect of the wind, he shot his second arrow even more carefully than his first. This time, his arrow landed in the very center of the target.

The crowd cheered loudly. "You cannot beat that shot, Locksley," Prince John said with an insulting smile.

"I will notch his shaft for him," Locksley replied and let fly his arrow. It struck Hubert's arrow and split it in two. The crowd was speechless at this show of skill, for they had never seen such a fine shot.

Even Prince John had to admire Locksley's skill, and he decided to use it to his own advantage. "I will reward you with great wealth if you will join my service," he offered.

"Pardon me, noble Prince," said Locksley, "but I have vowed that if I ever take service, it will be with your royal brother, King Richard." So saying, the mysterious archer stepped into the crowd and was seen no more.

The tournament was a great success, but Prince John is very worried about the return of King Richard. In fact, he's so caught up with planning what he'll do when his brother shows up, he forgets to arrange the marriage of De Bracy and Lady Rowena. But De Bracy hasn't forgotten! He is determined to make Rowena his wife, even if he has to take matters into his own hands.

Late that night, Waldemar Fitzurse met Maurice De Bracy in the hallway of Castle Ashby. De Bracy was disguised as a forest outlaw in a green tunic, green tights, and a leather cap. He had a horn slung over his shoulder, a bundle of arrows stuck in his belt, and a bow in his hand.

"What on earth are you doing?" Fitzurse said in surprise. "This is no time for a costume party, not now when Prince John is planning his future."

"I have been planning my own future," De Bracy said calmly.

"What future could possibly lead you to dress as an outlaw?" Fitzurse demanded.

"I am planning to get me a wife," De Bracy replied. "I will attack Cedric and his party, that herd of Saxon sheep. They left the castle tonight. I will carry the lovely Rowena away from them. Since I will be seen as a forest outlaw, none of the blame will fall upon me! Is my plan not clever?"

"It is," Fitzurse agreed, "much too clever for you to have thought of it! Tell me, who gave you this idea?"

"Sir Brian," De Bracy admitted. "He and his followers are going to help me. It will be the work of just a few hours. Then I will return to Prince John's service and be ready to help him face whatever the future holds."

What a rat! De Bracy's wicked plans spell danger for Rowena and everyone traveling with her.

7
The Hermit of Copmanhurst

And what about the mysterious Black Knight. He appeared out of nowhere to help Ivanhoe at the tournament, then vanished just as quickly. Let's find out what has become of him.

While the heralds were calling for him at the tournament, the man known as the Black Knight was already far away, riding through the woods at a quick and steady pace. He spent the night at a small inn, where he heard the story of what had happened at Ashby after he left.

The next morning, the Black Knight set off early. He intended to travel far that day, but he soon became lost in the twisting woodland paths. By nightfall, both he and his horse were exhausted and far from any town where they might find shelter.

The sun sank behind the hills, and the knight knew looking for a path in the darkness would be foolish. But he had to find food and shelter. So he decided to trust his horse. Letting go of the reins, he allowed the animal to choose the best path to take. **I like this guy! He knows that animals are good at nosing out food and shelter, so he's letting the horse decide where they should go!**

The path his horse chose was narrow at first but soon grew wider, and before long the travelers came to a field bordered by a large rock. Leaning against the rock was a simple hut built of tree trunks. Before it stood a tree, stripped of its branches and with a piece of wood tied across it near the top, which made a simple cross. A fountain of the purest water trickled from the rock, filling a shallow stone basin before it flowed into the forest. Beside the fountain were the ruins of a chapel. Its roof had fallen in, but the walls and bell tower still stood. A weather-beaten bell chimed cheerfully in the stillness of the woods.

The whole scene was so lovely and peaceful, it delighted the eyes of the weary Black Knight. Surely he would find lodging for the night here, since it was a special duty of hermits to offer hospitality to weary travelers.

The Black Knight stepped confidently to the door and knocked loudly. He waited a long time before receiving an answer.

"Go away, whoever you are," a voice called from inside the hut. "Do not disturb a servant of God in his evening prayers."

"Worthy father," the Black Knight said, "I am only a poor wanderer who has lost his way in these woods. I ask you for your charity and hospitality."

"I don't have enough food to share with a dog," the hermit replied. "Go away from here, I say!"

"How can I find my way through these woods in

the dark?" the Black Knight asked in exasperation. "If you cannot offer me food and shelter, at least give me directions to the main road."

"The road is easy to find," the voice called through the door. "Follow this path through the swamp until you reach the ford. **A ford is a place where it's possible to wade across a river or stream.** Rain has not fallen for some time, so you probably won't be washed away when you cross there. Be careful walking beside the water, though, for there is a cliff there, and I've heard the path has given away in a few places. Then—"

"A swamp, a flooded ford, and a cliff?" the Black Knight interrupted, scarcely able to believe his ears. "I tell you, Sir Hermit, there is no way I will risk my life on such a dangerous road tonight! You have no right to refuse shelter to a traveler in distress. Either open this door right now, or I will beat it down!" To prove the truth of his words, he kicked the door so hard the whole building shook.

"Patience, patience, I am coming," the hermit grumbled, "though you may be sorry at having disturbed me."

A few moments later, the door swung open. The hermit, a large, powerfully built man wearing a simple gown and hood, stood before the knight. In one hand he held a torch; in the other, a stout wooden club. He seemed about to strike the weary traveler, but then he saw the Black Knight's spurs and helmet gleaming in the torch light and thought better of it.

"Come in, Sir Knight," the hermit said grumpily. "I thought you were a robber, and that is why I did not want to let you in."

The Black Knight glanced around the simple room, which held nothing but a bed of leaves, a roughly carved crucifix, a table, and two stools. "Your poverty should be protection enough against anyone who might want to rob you," he commented.

The two men sat down at the table. The Black Knight looked at his guest and thought he had never seen such a strong-looking man.

"Tell me, good hermit," the knight said, "what am I to have for supper?"

The hermit reached over to a shelf on the wall and set down a dish containing a few handfuls of dried peas. The Black Knight picked up some pieces and began to chew on the dry, tasteless food. After a few moments, he choked, "May I have something to drink?"

"Of course," the hermit said. He placed a can of water before the knight. "This is from the spring outside my door," he explained. "It is the purest water around."

As he drank the water and continued to chew the dried peas, the knight could not help staring at his companion. The hermit looked nothing like a man who lived on peas and water. His body was so strong and his face so ruddy and plump, he must surely be getting his fill of fowl and venison.

"You seem to thrive mightily on this simple food and drink," the knight said at last. "You look more like a

Helllooo! Start flipping the pages and check out the action.... Woo-cha!

man who could win a wrestling match than one who does nothing but pray in the wilderness and live on peas and cold water. What is your name, good hermit?"

"People call me the Clerk of Copmanhurst," said the hermit, "though I am also known as Friar Tuck. What is your name?"

"People call me the Black Knight."

"Well, Sir Black Knight, I can see you do not like the simple fare I have offered you. You are more accustomed to the luxuries of cities and castles, are you not? One of my friends left me some food that may be more to your liking."

"I knew it!" the Black Knight exclaimed. "Let us see what your friend has given you."

Friar Tuck went to the far side of the hut and opened a small door in the wall. The tiny closet was lined with shelves. He brought out a huge meat pie, the largest one the Black Knight had ever seen.

The knight dug into the pie with his knife as soon as the Friar laid it on the table before him. "This is delicious!" he exclaimed as he stuffed his mouth with the tasty meat. Then he noticed the longing glances of his host and added, "Won't you join me? I cannot enjoy this pie if I have to eat it by myself while you watch."

"It is against my vows, but if it will help your conscience..." the hermit said. He plunged his hands into the pie. **Forks hadn't been invented yet!**

With two such hungry men feasting on it, the huge meat pie disappeared quickly. Indeed, even though the Black Knight was very hungry, the hermit ate even more than the knight did!

"Good hermit," the Black Knight said when every

last crumb was gone, "I would bet that the same friend who left you this tasty pie has also supplied you with some wine. I'm sure you have forgotten all about it, since your head is filled with nothing but prayers. Still, I wonder if you might search that closet once again." **It looks like the Black Knight has figured out that this hermit is not living the simple life he wants people to think he is!**

Friar Tuck smiled and went back to the closet. He returned carrying a bottle and two cups. Grinning at each other, the two men drank deeply.

"Good hermit," the Black Knight said, "I cannot but marvel that such a strong, hearty man would live a simple, quiet life in the woods. I know these woods are filled with many fine herds of the king's deer. Surely you have gone out at midnight, once or twice, and shot a deer or two?"

"Those are dangerous words," Friar Tuck warned. "If I were to do such a thing, even my hermit's gown would not save me from hanging. Speak no more of such things, or I will make your stay here a painful one." **He's right. Hunting the king's deer was against the law for anyone other than the king and his friends.**

"By my faith, you are the most curious man I have ever met!" the Black Knight exclaimed. "If you are going to threaten me, you should know that fighting is my business, and I am very good at it."

"I respect your bravery, Sir Knight," Friar Tuck said. "But I tell you this: If you were to take up arms against me, I would give you such a penance that you would not suffer the sin of curiosity for the next 12 months!" **Hermits and priests had the power to assign penance—a prayer**

"Name your weapons," the Black Knight said, "and I will accept your challenge."

"A good hermit has no weapons," Friar Tuck said. "But what do you think of these?" So saying, he walked to another closet and took out several swords and shields. Peering over the hermit's shoulder, the Black Knight could also see two or three longbows, a crossbow, and a great number of arrows. A harp was also sheltered inside.

"I shall ask no more questions," the Black Knight said, "for the contents of that closet have answered them all. I see a weapon there on which I would prefer to prove my skill." So saying, he reached into the closet and pulled out the harp.

Friar Tuck was more than happy to agree. "Fill your cup, then, and let us sing, drink, and be merry. I promise you, if you can sing a fine song, there will be a tasty meat pie waiting for you at Copmanhurst for as long as I live here."

So saying, the good hermit tuned the harp and handed it to the knight. Soon the little hut was filled with rollicking songs and laughter.

Friar Tuck may not be the simple hermit he pretends to be, but he certainly is a lot of fun to be around. Let's leave him and the Black Knight to their songs and check back with the other characters in the story.

8
In the Care of a Stranger

We now know what happened to the Black Knight after he left the tournament. Let's find out what happened to Ivanhoe and Cedric.

When Cedric the Saxon saw his son faint at Rowena's feet, his first thought was to go to his wounded son and make sure his servants gave the young knight the best of care. He almost called to Ivanhoe, but the words choked in Cedric's throat, and he could not bring himself to acknowledge the son whom he had disinherited, especially in front of such a huge crowd. By the time the crowd had gone home, it was too late. Ivanhoe had disappeared.

Cedric ordered his servants to find out what had happened to Ivanhoe. But all anyone knew was that the knight was in the care of an unnamed lady who had been among the spectators. All that remained of him at the tournament was the spot of blood on the ground where he had fainted.

Although Cedric did not know it, the woman who

was caring for his son was Rebecca, daughter of Isaac of York. She was a kindhearted young woman who had studied the healing arts. **In the Middle Ages, doctors relied more on superstition than on medicine to heal sickness and injury. But Rebecca knows how to use herbs and other natural remedies to heal ill or wounded people.** She was eager to help this man who, when disguised as a Palmer, had saved her father from Sir Brian's men. She had Ivanhoe taken to the house where she and her father were staying at Ashby and cared for him herself.

When Ivanhoe awoke that night, he was weak and sick from the injury he had suffered at the tournament. He was also very surprised to find himself in a room he had never seen before. When Rebecca stepped forward to check his wound, Ivanhoe could not help but stare at her beautiful dark hair and brilliant eyes. "Gentle maiden," he whispered, "most noble woman—"

Rebecca hushed him quickly. "Do not give me the honor of calling me noble," she said. "I am but a humble Jewish girl, the daughter of Isaac of York, to whom you were so kind."

Ivanhoe was dazzled by Rebecca's beauty and grace. Rebecca's eyes, fringed by long, dark lashes, seemed to him to be like twin evening stars, dancing behind a wispy curtain of fleeting clouds. But the news that she was Jewish restored him to his senses, for he could not allow himself to be attracted to a woman whose religion was different from his. Rebecca knew that as well, yet she could not help but sigh with disappointment when she saw that her words changed Ivanhoe's tenderness into polite gratitude for her help and care.

"How soon till I can ride to battle again?" Ivanhoe asked.

"If you were in the care of any other doctor, I would say it would take at least a month," Rebecca said. "But I am skilled in the healing arts. If you are patient and do as I tell you, I can have you on your feet in eight days!"

"That is good news!" Ivanhoe exclaimed. "This is no

time for me to be bedridden. If you can have me on my feet in eight days, I will give you as much gold as my helmet can hold."

"I would rather you grant me a favor than give me the gold you speak of," Rebecca said.

"Name it, and I will do it," Ivanhoe quickly agreed.

"All I ask is that you believe that a Jew may do a good service for a Christian without hoping for a reward. The deed is done simply because it is the right thing to do."

"I would never doubt it," Ivanhoe said. "I trust you completely. And now, good Rebecca, please tell me what happened at the tournament after I fell ill. What happened to the party of Saxons, Cedric, and the lovely Lady Rowena?"

"I can tell you that Cedric and Athelstane have left Ashby and started for home," Rebecca answered. "The Lady Rowena was with them. Now you must be quiet and rest."

By the next day, Ivanhoe was far from well enough to travel. His wound would need more time to heal. However, Isaac and Rebecca were eager to reach their home in York. They placed Ivanhoe in a litter so he could travel despite his injury. **A litter was like a covered stretcher carried by horses. It was a common way for people to travel if they were wealthy or too sick to ride on horseback.** Then the three of them, along with six soldiers hired to escort them, set off along the forest paths that led away from Ashby.

Rebecca and Ivanhoe aren't the only ones to set off on a journey. Cedric, Athelstane, and Rowena, along with their servants Wamba and Gurth, are also on the way home. Now the paths of our travelers are about to cross.

Unable to find his son, Cedric and his companions began the journey home. After some time, they reached the edge of a thick forest. Many men would have been afraid to venture into the woods, for the trees often hid dangerous bands of robbers who would not hesitate to attack any traveler unlucky enough to meet them. But Cedric was confident that he had enough men in his party for protection, and so the group plunged into the darkness of the forest.

They had not gone far when they heard someone crying for help. Hurrying forward, the travelers found a litter lying on the ground. Seated beside it were an old man and his daughter—Isaac and Rebecca!

Isaac explained that he and his daughter had hired six men to accompany them and their wounded friend to York. But when the men heard tales of robbers in the woods, they fled—and took the group's horses and mules with them! Isaac and Rebecca were stranded in the gloomy forest, with no way of protecting themselves from the bandits lurking in the trees.

"Will you allow us to join your party and travel under your safeguard?" Isaac asked Cedric. "If you do, we will be forever grateful."

Cedric did not really want the Jews to join his party, but he didn't want to leave them in such trouble either. "I will lend you two of our horses and two soldiers so you can travel on in safety," he offered.

Rowena agreed with her guardian's suggestion. But Rebecca stepped forward suddenly and bowed before her. "My lady," the Jewish girl said, "I beg you to allow us to travel under your protection. I ask this not for myself or even for the sake of my poor old father. I ask it in the name of one who is very dear to you. I tell you, if anything bad should happen to the sick man who travels in that litter, you will regret it for the rest of your life."

The noble and solemn manner in which Rebecca made her request moved Rowena deeply. She immediately decided to help her. "The man is old and feeble," she said to Cedric, "the maiden young and fair, and their friend in grave danger. We cannot leave them in such trouble. Let them ride with us."

Cedric finally agreed, and the group once more set off through the forest.

Rowena doesn't know it, but we know Rebecca's sick friend is none other than Ivanhoe himself! Rebecca and Isaac feel safe in Cedric's company—but are they?

9
Ambushed!

Just about every good adventure story set in the Middle Ages has a damsel in distress—a sweet, innocent lady who is in big trouble. Our story has two—Rowena and Rebecca. Trouble is waiting for them just around the corner!

Cedric and his fellow travelers headed deeper into the forest. The narrow path they followed led over a brook edged by swampy, overgrown banks that could easily hide robbers. It was not a safe place to be, and the group hurried through as fast as they could.

They were not fast enough, however. Most of the group had just crossed the brook when they were attacked! Sir Brian, De Bracy, and their men, disguised as bandits, swarmed from the trees and surrounded the little group from all directions.

Cedric managed to kill one of the kidnappers. Cedric fought with such force that his next blow knocked the sword right out of his hand. Without a weapon he was quickly taken prisoner. Athelstane was disarmed and pulled from his horse before he could even draw his weapon. The other members of the group were also taken prisoner, with the exception of Wamba and Gurth. The two slaves somehow managed to disappear into the woods.

As Wamba and Gurth escaped through the trees, a

man suddenly jumped into their path and commanded them to stop. At first Wamba thought he was another of the bandits but then recognized Locksley, the bold man who had won the archery contest at Ashby.

When Locksley learned what had happened, he quickly offered his help. "You are both faithful servants of Cedric, friend to all who are of Saxon blood. Come with me while I gather my men so we can go to his aid."

Locksley and his new friends hurried through the forest. Along the way, they met many of Locksley's band of outlaws. All vowed to help rescue Cedric and his friends. Locksley also sought out Friar Tuck, the well-fed hermit of Copmanhurst. He was as good a fighter as any of Locksley's band. As luck would have it, the Black Knight was still at the Friar's hut and also agreed to join the rescue mission.

While the rescuers continued to gather their forces, Cedric and his party were being hurried through the woods by their captors. They were headed to Torquilstone, a castle belonging to a friend of De Bracy's. There De Bracy intended to hold them captive until he could wed Rowena.

Sir Brian and De Bracy walked ahead of the others, conferring in whispers. "Soon we will arrive at Torquilstone," De Bracy said. "What do you mean to do there? I warn you," he added jealously, "I plan to make Rowena my bride, and I will not let anyone stop me."

"I care not for your blue-eyed beauty," Sir Brian responded. "There is one in that party who pleases me more than she does."

"Who? One of Lady Rowena's maids?" De Bracy said with a laugh.

"Of course not," Sir Brian said, insulted that his friend would think a mighty knight such as he would be interested in a mere servant.

De Bracy stared at him in surprise. "Surely you don't mean the Jewish girl?" he asked.

"I do," Sir Brian said. "Ever since I saw her when we ambushed the group in the woods, I haven't been able to stop thinking about her. Rebecca is so beautiful, I must have her for my own. Nothing and no one will stop me!"

De Bracy could see that nothing would change his friend's mind on this matter. The group continued on to the fortress of Torquilstone. The prisoners were rudely ushered into the heavily fortified castle, each to a separate room. There they waited, fearful of what their captors meant to do to them.

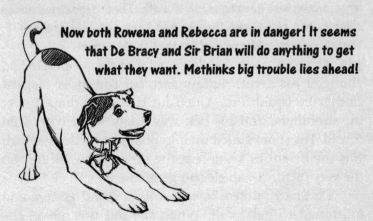

Now both Rowena and Rebecca are in danger! It seems that De Bracy and Sir Brian will do anything to get what they want. Methinks big trouble lies ahead!

10
Prisoners in the Tower

All the prisoners are very nervous. They can't imagine why they've been captured or what might happen to them. No one is in more danger than Lady Rowena and Rebecca. Let's see what their captors have in mind.

The room in which Lady Rowena was being held had once been elegant, but the passage of time had caused a great deal of decay and neglect. The tapestries on the wall were faded from the sun and tattered by age, and everything was covered with a thick layer of dust. **No castle was complete without a tapestry—a large, woven wall hanging made of cloth. These tapestries added color to the room, and they helped keep out cold drafts too. There's nothing colder or draftier than an old castle!**

At about noon, De Bracy entered the room. He had changed his green outlaw garb for the most elegant clothes he could find. A rich fur cloak was draped over his shoulders, and his belt was finely sewn with gold thread. His shoes curled up into points at the toes, which was the height of fashion at the time. All in all, he was the very picture of an elegant gentleman.

De Bracy saluted Rowena with a grand gesture and motioned to her to sit. When she did not move, the knight reached out to lead her to a seat. But Rowena still refused his offer. "If I am in the presence of my jailer, Sir

Knight, I would rather remain standing until I learn my fate," she said coolly.

"Alas, fair Rowena," De Bracy responded, "I am your captive, not your jailer, for I have fallen prisoner to your beauty."

"I don't know you, sir, but I know that no true knight would intrude on an unprotected maiden as you have," Rowena replied with great dignity.

"My name is De Bracy," the knight replied. "Surely you have heard heralds and minstrels sing my praises in their tales of great battles."

> Minstrels wrote and performed songs about the great heroes of the day.

"I'll let the heralds and minstrels praise you," Rowena said scornfully. "Tell me, which of them will record the memorable conquest you have made here—overcoming old men and maidens who could not defend themselves and carrying them off against their will?"

"When I saw your beauty, I could not help myself," De Bracy admitted.

Rowena was growing impatient at De Bracy's ridiculous compliments. "Please stop talking like a minstrel," she snapped. "Such polite language, when it is used to cover up a foul deed, is like dressing a clown in a knight's clothes. It would be more fitting for you to have kept your outlaw dress, since your actions were those of a common criminal."

De Bracy had been sure that his fine words and

charming manner would win over this fair maiden, and Rowena's harsh words made him angry. "If you want bold language, I will give it to you," he growled. "You shall never leave this castle unless you leave it as my wife. Consider yourself lucky. I will make you richer than any of these Saxon churls could."

"You dare to talk to me this way only because no one is here to protect me," Rowena said. "I could never marry anyone who held my Saxon people in such low esteem," she added, angry at De Bracy's insulting words. "I shall wed no one who does not respect my heritage."

"You mean Ivanhoe," De Bracy said scornfully. "He is in my power at this very moment and is in no position to come to your aid."

"Ivanhoe is here?" Rowena said in surprise.

"Of course," De Bracy replied. "He is the injured man who rode in the Jews' litter."

"If what you say is true," Rowena said nervously, "then the laws of chivalry demand that you release him upon payment of a ransom." **Captured knights commonly bought release by giving their captors money or treasure.**

De Bracy laughed. "Do you really think I would let my rival for your affections escape so easily? No, fair lady, this is how it shall be: If you become my bride, Ivanhoe will go free— unharmed. But if you refuse me, then Ivanhoe will die."

"Save him, for the love of Heaven!" Rowena cried.

"I will—as soon as you agree to marry me." As if his

threat was not horrible enough, De Bracy added, "Your guardian, Cedric, is also my prisoner. His fate also depends on your answer to me." **What a rat! De Bracy is threatening to kill Rowena's true love AND the man who is like a father to her unless she agrees to marry De Bracy!**

Until now, Rowena had tried her best to be brave and strong and not let her captor see how frightened she was. But this final threat was too much for her. She burst into tears.

Even De Bracy, as hard-hearted as he was, could not stand to see this beautiful woman cry. He paced back and forth nervously, begging her to stop. "I cannot bear to see such beautiful eyes drowned in tears," he said. But his attempts at comfort did nothing to stop Rowena's crying.

Just then, the blast of a bugle cut through the air. "Something must be wrong," De Bracy said. Relieved that the interruption rescued him from such an unpleasant situation, he hurried from the room, leaving Rowena to her sorrows.

In another part of the castle, Rebecca was still waiting to hear her fate. She expected something terrible would happen, for she well knew the hostility most folk had for the Jewish people. But she also knew she had the strength to face whatever happened.

She stood, trembling and pale, as a step sounded on the stairs. The door of her chamber swung open, and a tall man, dressed as an outlaw, walked slowly into the room. His cap was pulled down and his cloak pulled up to cover his face. He stood silently, until Rebecca could stand it no longer.

She unclasped two jeweled bracelets from her arms and held them out to the stranger. "Take these as ransom for myself and my aged father," she pleaded. "I beg you, have mercy!"

"Fair flower," replied the man, "these jewels are nothing compared with the diamonds of your eyes and the pearls of your teeth. I have always valued beauty over wealth. Your ransom must be paid by love and beauty. I will accept no other coin."

"You are no outlaw," Rebecca said. "No outlaw would refuse these riches, and no outlaw has a high-born accent such as yours. You are a Norman knight!"

"You have guessed the truth," said Sir Brian, dropping the cloak from his face. "I am a Knight Templar, not an outlaw. And I do not desire your jewels."

"What do you want from me, if not my wealth?" Rebecca asked.

"I want you for my own. Your beauty is all I desire," Sir Brian replied, laughing. "You are my captive and subject to my will."

"If you lay one finger on me, I will proclaim your villainy from one end of the land to the other!" Rebecca cried. "Every member of the Knights Templar will know what you have done and how you have dishonored your order. No one will want to associate with you after they hear what you have done."

"You are keen-witted," Sir Brian said, for he knew she was right. "But your voice must be loud enough to be heard beyond these castle walls. And you will not leave here unless you leave in my arms."

"I spit on you and defy you!" Rebecca shouted

angrily. "There is still one way for me to escape, and I will take it!" So saying, she threw open a window and stood on the ledge. The ground was very far below her. "Come no nearer, Sir Knight," Rebecca warned. "One step closer and I will plunge from this ledge, and my body will be crushed against the stones below!" **Rebecca would rather kill herself than have anything to do with this barbaric knight.**

Sir Brian was so surprised at Rebecca's threat, he stood perfectly still. He could have stood firm against her tears and her pleas. But he so admired her bravery and strong will, he found he could not fight her.

"Come down," he said at last. "I swear I will not harm you."

"I do not trust you," Rebecca said, not moving from the window ledge. "How do I know you will not break your promise?"

"May my name, Sir Brian de Bois-Guilbert, be dishonored forever if I do you any harm," Sir Brian vowed. "I have broken many laws, but I have never broken my word."

Rebecca climbed down from the ledge but remained standing close to the window. "Come no closer," she warned her captor. Her anger and determination made her even more appealing in Sir Brian's eyes.

"Let there be peace between us, Rebecca," Sir Brian said.

"There can be peace only if you come no closer to me," Rebecca replied.

The sound of a bugle broke the uneasy silence between them. "That call announces something that may require my presence," Sir Brian said as he headed for the door. "Farewell. I will return soon, for I wish to talk more with you." With those words, he was gone.

Rebecca is really brave and more than a match for this knight! But what does that bugle cry mean?

11
The Greatest Gift

When Sir Brian reached the hall of the castle, he found De Bracy already there. "I suppose your courtship has been disturbed by this bugle cry, as has mine," De Bracy said. "I hope you had better luck than I did." He sighed. "Lady Rowena must have heard that I cannot stand the sight of a woman's tears. I have never seen such an overflowing of the eyes!"

"And I have never seen such pride and determination as I did in Rebecca," Sir Brian replied. "But never mind that now. Is there a messenger? What news does he bring?"

A few moments later, a servant brought the knights a letter. Sir Brian opened it and read it aloud. "It says, 'I, Wamba, jester to Cedric of Rotherwood, and I, Gurth, swineherd to Cedric, with the aid of our friends Locksley and the Black Knight, declare that you have wrongly seized Cedric, along with Lady Rowena, Athelstane, Isaac and Rebecca of York, and a wounded knight. If they are not returned safely to us within an hour of your receiving this note, we will attack the castle and destroy you.'"

De Bracy burst into laughter. "That is the most ridiculous challenge I have ever heard."

"There are at least 200 men outside the walls, my lord," said the servant who had brought in the message. He was obviously nervous.

"Just peasants!" Sir Brian said scornfully. "One knight is worth 20 of such common folk. I will send a message back to those rude people that will cool their fire." He quickly sat down and wrote a note: "Cedric and Athelstane will be executed tomorrow morning and their heads placed on the walls to show all men what we think of you who plan their rescue. If you want to help them, send a priest into the castle to hear their confessions." **A man who was going to be executed, or killed, had the right to talk to a priest before he died. The priest would hear his confession and try to help him face death with a clear conscience.** The message was sent, and the knights sat back to see what the response might be.

The rescuers were camped under a huge oak tree the distance of about three arrow flights from the castle of Torquilstone. When they received the answer from Sir Brian, the Black Knight read its threatening contents to the others.

"There is nothing to do but tear down the castle walls with our bare hands!" Gurth shouted when he heard what Sir Brian planned to do to his master.

"If only one of us could get into the castle and see what is happening there," said the Black Knight. He turned to Friar Tuck. "Friar Tuck, will you go to the castle and hear the confessions of the doomed men?"

"Not I," the Friar replied. "I have taken off my friar's robes to wear an outlaw's dress. I am a man of action and do not wish to miss the fighting by playing priest."

"I see that the fool must be the one to put his neck in the spot where wiser men dare not go," Wamba said. "Let me wear the friar's black robe; I will go to the castle in his place."

Everyone agreed, and Wamba was soon dressed and ready to go. Off he walked, imitating the solemn, stately step of a man whose life was filled with nothing but prayer and good deeds.

When Wamba approached the castle gate, he told the guard, "I have come to hear the confessions of the unhappy prisoners within this castle." Those words gained him entry, and he was soon taken to the room where Cedric and Athelstane were being held.

"Blessings upon you," Wamba said to the men. He spoke in a disguised voice, still pretending to be a priest.

"And on you," Cedric replied. He could not understand why a priest had come to see him, and he asked, "What brings you here?"

"To bid you to prepare yourselves for death," the "priest" replied.

"Impossible!" Cedric cried. "Even these men would not dare commit such wickedness!"

"Alas, to stop them would be like trying to stop a runaway horse with a bridle of silk thread," Wamba replied.

"I am ready," Athelstane said, "and will do my best to walk to my death as calmly as I would walk to dinner."

"Let us make our confessions, then," Cedric said, resigned to his fate.

"Wait a moment," said Wamba in his regular voice.

"Look before you leap into the dark."

"I know that voice!" Cedric cried. "It is my jester!"

Wamba threw back his hood to reveal his face. "If you take a fool's advice, you will not be here long," he told Cedric. "Take this friar's robe and march quickly out of the castle, leaving me in your place."

"Leave you here in my place?" Cedric said in astonishment. "But you will be hanged!"

"Let them do what they will," Wamba said calmly. "I trust I can hang as well as you, even though I am a slave and you are a noble."

"There is only one way I will do as you ask," Cedric said. "Change clothes with Athelstane so he may go free instead."

"Why should I do that?" Wamba replied. "It is right for me to save my master, but I would truly be a fool to die for a man who is practically a stranger to me."

"But his forefathers were of royal blood!" Cedric protested.

"His forefathers are strangers to me too," Wamba said.

"Do as he asks, Cedric," Athelstane said. "I would rather remain in this prison for a week without food than take the place of a man whose servant is willing to die for him."

"I came to save my master," Wamba insisted. "I will hang for no man but him."

Cedric finally agreed. "Farewell, noble Athelstane. And farewell, Wamba, whose brave heart makes up for his foolish head," Cedric said. "I will save you or return to die with you! Farewell!" Eyes filling with tears, he made his way out of the castle to safety.

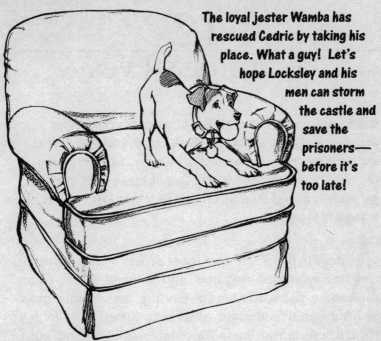

The loyal jester Wamba has rescued Cedric by taking his place. What a guy! Let's hope Locksley and his men can storm the castle and save the prisoners— before it's too late!

12
Ivanhoe's Eyes

Cedric escapes and makes his way to Locksley's camp. After deciding on a plan of attack, the Black Knight, Locksley, Cedric, and the others approach the castle. De Bracy and Sir Brian see the outlaw army advancing toward Torquilstone's walls, and they get ready to defend themselves. Hold on to your hats—the battle is about to begin!

After Sir Brian left her, Rebecca was sent to care for the wounded Ivanhoe, and she was in his room when the battle began. Finding herself once more at Ivanhoe's side brought comfort to Rebecca—even at a time when danger was all around. As she felt his pulse and asked how he was feeling, her voice was softer and warmer than she had expected it to be, and the touch of her hand against his arm pleased her. Only when Ivanhoe asked, "Is it you, gentle maiden?" in a cool, polite voice did Rebecca come to her senses. "He does not feel the same way for me as I do for him," Rebecca regretfully reminded herself.

Suddenly the castle echoed with the heavy steps of knights in clanking armor and the frantic shouts of De Bracy and Sir Brian giving orders to their men. Ivanhoe could scarcely lie still as the tension and excitement grew stronger, yet the seriousness of his injury would not allow him to do more than sit up in bed.

"If only I could drag myself out of this bed and over to yonder window, at least I could see what is happening!" he said impatiently. "Even if I could shoot one arrow through the window, I could at least strike a blow for our cause. But it is useless—I don't have the strength."

"Lie back," Rebecca said with concern. "You will only injure yourself. I myself will stand at the window and tell you what is happening."

"You must not!" Ivanhoe exclaimed. "A stray arrow could strike you. The danger is too great."

But Rebecca had already moved to the window. "Dear Rebecca, you must not expose yourself to injury and death," Ivanhoe begged her. "I would be miserable to the end of my days if I should put you in such danger. At least take that shield from the wall and cover yourself for some protection."

Rebecca did as she was asked. "The edge of the woods is lined with archers," she reported.

"What banner do they fight under?" Ivanhoe asked. **In the Middle Ages, each army carried a banner displaying a symbol of its leader on it. Keeping an eye on that banner helped soldiers stay together in the confusion of battle.**

"None," Rebecca said. "But their leader is a knight clad all in black."

Knights bearing huge shields and other defenses rushed toward Torquilstone's walls, while a row of men behind them prepared to fire arrows at the castle's defenders. "God, forgive the creatures you have made!" Rebecca whispered, horrified at the violence before her.

A shrill bugle signaled that the assault was about to begin. Soon the air was filled with arrows and other missiles, along with the shouts and screams of men. Locksley's men fought hard, but so did the defenders.

"What do you see now, Rebecca?" Ivanhoe asked eagerly.

"Nothing but a cloud of arrows flying so thick as to dazzle my eyes," Rebecca replied.

"I cannot bear it!" Ivanhoe cried in frustration. "How can I lie here while the battle that will give me freedom or death goes on without me? Tell me, Rebecca, where is the Black Knight?"

"I can't see him."

"Coward!" Ivanhoe exclaimed. "Does he run from the field when the fighting is hardest?"

"No, I see him now!" Rebecca cried. "He is leading a group of men close to the outermost wall of the castle, the wooden wall before the gate. They are chopping down the wall with axes! But Sir Brian and his men are beating them back! They are fighting hand to hand now." She looked away, unable to watch the violence any longer.

"Look again, Rebecca," Ivanhoe urged her.

The maiden took up her watch again, only to cry out, "He is down! He is down!"

"Who?"

"The Black Knight," answered Rebecca faintly. Then she shouted joyfully, "No, he is on his feet again and fights as if the strength of 20 men was in his arm. He is battering the gate with his huge ax. Stones and wooden beams are being thrown all around him, yet he pays them no more mind than if they were feathers!"

"I thought there was but one man in England who could perform such a deed," Ivanhoe said wonderingly, awed by the Black Knight's courage and strength.

"The gate shakes," continued Rebecca, "it is splintered—it is down! The Black Knight's men have taken the outer wall!"

Silence fell over the castle. "It is over for now," Rebecca reported. "Our friends are resting in the shelter of the wall."

"Surely our friends will not abandon the rescue when they've come this far," Ivanhoe said joyfully. "I will put my faith in the Black Knight. I'd endure ten years' captivity to fight one day by that good knight's side!"

"Indeed, it is fearful, yet magnificent, to behold how the arm and heart of one man can triumph over hundreds," Rebecca agreed. "I can scarcely bear to watch the fighting, yet I cannot tear my eyes away. But how can you hope to fight again when you have not yet recovered from the wound you suffered at Ashby?"

"It is impossible for a knight to feel otherwise," Ivanhoe explained. "The love of battle is the food upon which a knight lives."

"What good is that, when battle brings nothing but death and suffering?" Rebecca asked him. "What is left to reward you for all the tears your deeds have caused?"

"Glory," Ivanhoe responded without hesitation. "Glory and the ideal of chivalry that leads a true knight to fight for justice and honor." He lay back upon his bed, exhausted from the excitement of the battle. Soon he was fast asleep.

Rebecca stared down at Ivanhoe for a long time. "Is it a crime that I should look upon him?" she whispered. "Who knows when he may ride into battle again and find his death there. This may be the last time I see his fair features filled with the spark of his bold spirit." Rebecca shook her head, surprised at the feelings Ivanhoe was stirring up in her heart. "How can I care so much about this man?" she asked herself. "I must tear these feelings from my heart, even if doing so causes me to bleed to death!" With those words, Rebecca turned away and tried not to think about the dangers of the battle outside—and the dangers of her own forbidden feelings.

Rebecca is in love with Ivanhoe, but they can never have a future together. Not only are they from different religions and cultures, but Rebecca knows Ivanhoe is in love with Rowena. Love sure is complicated!

13
Victory!

A castle was designed to be hard to break into. Along with the high stone walls and towers that made up Torquilstone itself, the building was surrounded by an outer wall. Locksley and his outlaws have broken through Torquilstone's outer wall, but they are only in the castle yard. They still need to fight their way into the castle itself.

After gathering up their courage, Cedric and the Black Knight made a dash for the back gate of the castle and began to pound on it with their axes. At the same time, Locksley and his outlaws bombarded the castle with arrow after arrow, so no one from the castle could stop the attack on the gate.

"Shame on you!" De Bracy called to his soldiers, who were afraid to show their faces and risk being killed. "You call yourselves knights? Get a pickax and chop away the stone over the gate so it falls on those two outlaws!"

Soon De Bracy and his men were hard at work, despite the danger from arrows. Suddenly the air began to fill with smoke. Sir Brian hurried up beside De Bracy and whispered, "All is lost, De Bracy. The castle is on fire!"

"How could that happen?" De Bracy said in astonishment.

"One of the outlaws sent a burning arrow into the

thatch of the roof. The thatch was so dry, it went up immediately. The flames have spread to the inside walls, and the whole west side of the castle is nothing but flames. I tried to put the fire out, but it is spreading too fast. There is no hope."

"What can we do?" said De Bracy.

"Take your men through the back gate. Only the Black Knight and Cedric the Saxon are there, and you should easily be able to overcome them. Meanwhile, I will charge from the main gate. Perhaps between us we can hold the outlaws at bay and still escape with our lives."

De Bracy quickly drew his men together and rushed to the back of the castle. There he found his men retreating from the wall. Two of them had been killed by arrows, and the rest had lost the heart to fight. Determined to escape, De Bracy pushed open the gate. But no sooner had he opened it than the Black Knight burst through.

De Bracy stepped forward to meet the Black Knight's challenge. His sword thrust against the Black Knight's heavy ax. The two parried back and forth until the walls rang with their blows. At last the Black Knight struck a blow so powerful that De Bracy was thrown headlong to the ground.

"Yield to me," the Black Knight demanded of his fallen foe. "Yield or you are a dead man!"

"I will not yield to an unknown conqueror," De Bracy said bravely. "Tell me your name."

The Black Knight leaned over and slowly whispered in De Bracy's ear, "King Richard is back in England." De

Bracy's face betrayed his shock. "I yield to you," he mumbled.

"Go to the wall and wait for me there," the Black Knight said with authority.

"Yes, but first there is something you should know," De Bracy said. "Wilfred of Ivanhoe is wounded and a prisoner in the burning castle. He will die if someone does not help him."

"Wilfred of Ivanhoe!" the Black Knight exclaimed. "Every man in the castle shall answer to me if one hair of his head is harmed. Show me where he is."

De Bracy pointed up the stairs and the Black Knight hurried away.

Meanwhile, the smoke was growing thick in Ivanhoe's room. "How can we save ourselves from the fire?" Rebecca cried in panic. "We will be trapped here by the flames."

"Fly from here, Rebecca, and save your life," Ivanhoe told her.

"I will not leave you," Rebecca answered firmly. "We shall die or be saved together."

At that moment, the door of the room flew open and Sir Brian ran in. He was a horrible sight, for his armor was broken and bloody and his face was black with smoke.

"I have put myself in great danger to save you," he said to Rebecca. "There is but one way out. Come with me."

"Alone I will not follow you," Rebecca told him. "If you have any heart at all, save this wounded knight! And save my poor old father, whom you also hold prisoner in this castle."

"A knight can face his own fate, and I don't care about an old man. I care only about you. Come with me to safety."

"I would rather die in the flames than accept safety from you!" Rebecca cried.

"You have no choice," Sir Brian snarled. He seized the maiden and dragged her, screaming with terror, out of the room.

"Traitor! Stain of the Templars!" Ivanhoe shouted after him. "Set the maiden free, or I will have your heart's blood!" But Sir Brian paid no attention to the threats, for Ivanhoe's injury prevented him from rescuing Rebecca. Nothing could keep Sir Brian from carrying Rebecca away.

An instant later, the Black Knight entered the room. "I would not have found you had you not been shouting so loudly," he told Ivanhoe.

"Never mind me," Ivanhoe said. "Catch that false knight and save Rebecca and her father! Save the Lady Rowena! Find Cedric!"

"They will have their turn, but yours is first," the Black Knight said calmly. Seizing Ivanhoe, he carried the injured knight away as easily as Sir Brian had carried off Rebecca and delivered him to the safety of the back gate.

In the confusion of the fire and the battle, Cedric, with Gurth's help, was able to find Rowena, Athelstane, and Wamba. They all made their way safely out of the castle. As more of Locksley's men rushed in, Sir Brian clattered through the yard on horseback, swinging his

sword at anyone who tried to stop his escape. At the same time, he took great care that the woman he held prisoner should not be harmed.

When Athelstane saw that Sir Brian was carrying off a woman, he assumed the prisoner was Rowena. "I will rescue the fair maiden from that arrogant knight!" he shouted.

Snatching a weapon from the ground, Athelstane rushed forward with such fury that he quickly broke through all of Sir Brian's defenders. But Sir Brian was ready for him. Rising up in his stirrups, he struck a terrible blow to Athelstane's head. The Saxon warrior fell to the ground and lay still.

Shouting a victory cry, Sir Brian rode out of the castle. He spotted De Bracy standing beside the wall. "Come with me!" he called to his friend. "Save yourself!"

"I cannot," De Bracy answered. "I surrendered to the Black Knight and gave my word that I would not escape from here. King Richard and his hawks are back in England. You must flee and save yourself." **A hawk is a bird of prey. De Bracy is afraid he is in danger now that the true King and his men, whom he compares with hawks, have returned.**

"Let King Richard's hawks fly where they will," Sir Brian replied. "I will go to the Templars' headquarters at Templestowe and find safety there. No one would dare attack a house of God." He rode away, still holding Rebecca as his prisoner.

The towering flames had now triumphed over every obstacle. They rose to the sky in a huge beacon that could be seen far and wide through the countryside. Tower after tower crashed down, carrying the blazing roof and rafters along with them. At length, the last of the towers gave way and fell to earth with a terrific crash. The mighty fortress of Torquilstone was no more.

14
The Fate of Isaac

So Locksley's men have won the day. Ivanhoe has been rescued by the Black Knight and taken to a religious community where he can continue recovering from his wounds.

Locksley and his rescued friends made their way to a favorite spot in the woods—an aged oak tree about half a mile from the ruins of Torquilstone. Locksley settled himself in his usual seat at the base of the tree, with the Black Knight at his right hand and Cedric at his left. The other former prisoners of the castle gathered around them.

"Despite our victory today, I cannot help but be sad," Cedric said. "My noble friend Athelstane has been killed, and Lady Rowena and I must hurry back to his home at Coningsburgh and see to his funeral. But first I must reward my most loyal jester, Wamba." Moved by emotion, he turned and hugged the fool. "How can I reward a man who did not fear to face a death meant for me?"

"If you really wish to please me," Wamba said, "I beg you to free my friend Gurth, who has long been faithful to you. For many years now, he has been saving to buy his freedom. Will you not grant it to him for my sake?"

"I will," Cedric agreed. "Kneel, Gurth." The shepherd obeyed. "Slave you are no longer," Cedric said, laying his hand on Gurth's head. "You are a free man. I will give you a strip of land to farm from my own fields"

Gurth jumped to his feet and leaped high in the air, so great was his pleasure at being a free man and a landholder. "Quick, find me a blacksmith and a file so I may remove this slave's collar from around my neck," he cried. "Noble master," he said to Cedric, "you have doubled my strength by your gift, and I will fight doubly hard at your request. But Wamba," he added, turning to his friend, "why do you not ask for freedom for yourself?"

"I do not envy you your freedom," Wamba replied. "For the slave is safe by the hall fire while the freeman must go out to the field of battle to fight for his lord. Better a fool at a feast than a wise man at a fight, that's what I say."

Next, Cedric and Rowena thanked the Black Knight and Locksley. "How can I repay either of you for the help you have given us?" Cedric asked.

"For me," replied Locksley, "knowing I helped countrymen and a fair maiden in need is all the thanks I require. Perhaps," he added with a wink, "my deeds will make up for some of the deer my men and I have shot in your woods."

"I ask for nothing now," the Black Knight replied in turn. "But a time may come in the future when I will ask a favor of you."

"Ask anything and I shall do it," Cedric vowed, "in payment of the great debt I owe you."

Cedric and Rowena and their party then made ready to take Athelstane's body back to Coningsburgh. After they left, the Black Knight turned to his prisoner, De Bracy, and said, "You are free to leave here. I do not want to take revenge for the foul deeds you have done. But beware that great harm does not befall you in the future! I tell you, Maurice De Bracy—*beware*!"

De Bracy wasted no time in taking advantage of his freedom. He leaped onto the back of one of the horses and galloped off through the trees.

Suddenly, a voice rang out through the woods. "Make way, make way for a friar and his prisoner!" Friar Tuck strode through the trees, with Isaac of York trailing along behind him. "See, even this lowly priest has come away from battle with a treasure! Look who I found hiding in the ruins of the castle. I will not release him until he pays me a ransom, as the laws of chivalry allow."

As we mentioned before, a man who was captured in battle was allowed to win his freedom by paying a ransom. As a priest and an outlaw, Friar Tuck isn't really bound by the laws of chivalry the way a knight would be. But he really does expect Isaac to pay for his release.

"That seems fair," said Locksley. "Think, Isaac, how much are you willing to pay for your freedom? Meanwhile, I see my men have brought me yet another prisoner." He turned toward two of his men leading the brightly dressed figure of Prior Aymer between them.

"What is the meaning of this?" the Prior demanded when he saw Locksley. "Your men are demanding that

I—a man of the church—pay a ransom to win my freedom! How can you treat a priest this way?"

"A priest as rich as you should have no objection to paying for your freedom," said Locksley. **Why don't the outlaws respect the Prior? After all, he is a man of God. But in the Middle Ages, many of the important men of the church didn't act very holy. Despite their vows, they were fond of good times and good food, and they could be as cruel as any high-handed lord. The Prior is just such a man, and that's why the outlaws don't like him very much.**

One of Locksley's men said, "Wouldn't it be a good joke if the Prior should name Isaac's ransom, and Isaac should name the Prior's?"

The very ridiculousness of the idea amused Locksley. "It shall be done!" he announced. "Isaac, how much do you think this Prior can afford to pay us?"

Isaac thought for a moment. "From what I know of his wealth, I would say 600 crowns."

A crown was the name of a gold coin used in the Middle Ages. Six hundred crowns was a lot of money!

"What?" the Prior cried in outrage. But Locksley only laughed and said, "Now Prior, it is your turn. Name Isaac's ransom."

The Prior glared at the old man. "One thousand crowns," he said.

"I could never pay so much!" Isaac cried, greatly upset. "Please, sirs, be kind to a childless old man. You don't know what losing a beloved daughter is like. Oh, Rebecca, my dear child, I would give anything to know what has happened to you!"

"I know what became of your daughter," said one of the outlaws. "She was carried from the castle by the Knight Templar Sir Brian."

Isaac burst into tears at the terrible news. Locksley was moved to pity by his grief. "We will be gentle with you," he said to the old man. "Pay us a ransom of 500 hundred crowns, which must be delivered to us as soon as possible. You may keep the rest of your money to ransom your daughter from Sir Brian."

Isaac was cheered at the outlaw's generosity and at the thought that his beloved daughter might yet be restored to him. Even the Prior seemed to be moved by the old man's obvious love for his daughter.

"I know Sir Brian, and he may listen to what I have to say," the Prior told Isaac. "If you like, I will write a letter for you to take to him, encouraging the knight to release your daughter. Perhaps in exchange, you might give me some fine silver and gold for my church."

Isaac would have agreed to any price to rescue his daughter. Paper was quickly brought to the Prior. With the churchman's letter in hand, Isaac set off for the Templars' headquarters at Templestowe.

Will the Prior's letter help Isaac win his daughter's freedom?

15
Rebecca in Danger

While Isaac heads off to Templestowe to try to ransom his daughter, Rebecca, De Bracy has returned to Prince John's court. I wonder how the evil Prince will react when he discovers that big brother has come home?

Prince John and Waldemar Fitzurse listened in growing anger and fear to the story De Bracy told. "Torquilstone has fallen, and many of your loyal soldiers are dead," De Bracy said. "Sir Brian has fled to Templestowe to seek the protection of the Knights Templar. Worst of all," he added in a low voice, "King Richard is in England. I have seen and spoken to him."

Prince John turned pale and swayed on his feet. He grabbed the back of a bench to keep from falling and stood silently, worrying about the return of King Richard and what it would mean.

"That cannot be," said Fitzurse, equally shocked at the news that King Richard had returned.

"It is as true as truth itself," De Bracy insisted. "I was his prisoner and spoke with him."

"What do you mean, you were his prisoner?" Fitzurse asked in alarm. "Has he raised an army to march against Prince John?"

"No, he travels alone. He joined the outlaws only for the battle at Torquilstone."

"That is just like Richard," said Fitzurse. "He loves adventure and will wander all over the land in disguise, eager to test the strength of his arm for any good cause."

"Perhaps you and I should flee the country to ensure our safety," De Bracy suggested.

Prince John could not believe what he was hearing. "Do you mean to desert me so easily then?" he demanded. "How can you give up the wealth and honor I promised you?"

"Your Grace, don't you understand?" De Bracy said. "As soon as Richard returns to the throne, it will all be over for us. You must flee to safety."

"I will do no such thing," Prince John said proudly. "There is but one way to ensure our safety. You said Richard was traveling alone. Capturing him and making him our prisoner will be easy."

De Bracy and Fitzurse were not very eager to follow that plan. De Bracy was especially reluctant to pursue the man who had been merciful enough to grant him his freedom at Torquilstone. But Prince John appealed to the knights' greed and hunger for power, and at last the two men agreed to help. And so the three began to plan their attack on England's rightful King.

Prince John and his men are always causing trouble for someone! We'll leave them to their plotting and head for Templestowe, where Isaac has gone to seek his daughter's freedom.

Templestowe was surrounded by fair meadows and pastures. It was strong and well-defended. Two knights guarded the drawbridge, and more knights walked the walls, looking more like phantoms than soldiers in their black armor.

Isaac paused at the gate, not sure how he would gain entrance to such a place. At last, he simply asked one of the guards if he might speak with Sir Brian.

It was so unusual for a Jewish man to ask to speak to a Knight Templar that the guard sent word to the Grand Master of the order. The Grand Master was a stern man who would not put up with any nonsense. He was determined to make the Knights Templar obey the rules of their order without question. He listened carefully to the guard's report and thought hard about what to do.

The Grand Master knew Sir Brian well, and he was not at all sure that the knight was true to the spirit of the Templars. "Sir Brian has always been a moody, angry man," he reflected, "quick to cause trouble and argue against authority. I think it is best for me to hear what he has to do with this Jewish man." The Grand Master demanded that Isaac be brought before him.

Isaac was very nervous at being in the presence of someone so fierce and powerful. He trembled when the Grand Master boomed out, "What is your business with Sir Brian?"

"I bring him a letter from Prior Aymer," Isaac said in a trembling voice.

"Give it to me," the Grand Master demanded. "My duty is to make sure Sir Brian is not taking part in activities that might bring shame to our order." He broke the seal and read the letter. "Sir Brian," the letter stated, "I have heard that you escaped from Torquilstone and fled to your headquarters at Templestowe with a Jewish maiden whose beauty has bewitched you. I beg you to remember your vows and risk not the anger of your

Grand Master. Please allow the maiden's father, Isaac of York, to ransom his daughter and thus settle the matter to everyone's benefit."

"Please, sir," Isaac begged. "I would pay any price to free my daughter."

"Silence," the Grand Master roared, for he was very upset by what Sir Brian had done. "Sir Brian has taken a woman—a Jewish woman—and is keeping her here at Templestowe under my very nose? He knows that is against the rules of our order." He paused, musing. "I have heard of this Rebecca of York." He turned to Isaac. "Your daughter practices the healing arts, does she not?"

"Yes," Isaac replied. "Knight and peasant, lord and lady, all may bless the gift that Heaven has given her. Many will testify that Rebecca has healed them when all other human aid has proven useless."

"Only a witch could perform such miraculous cures," the Grand Master announced. "She has cast a spell on Sir Brian to make him fall in love with her. No, there will be no ransom, old man. We will put this girl on trial for her life, and if she is a witch, she shall die! Away with you!" he shouted at Isaac, who had paled and become faint when he heard the Grand Master's words. "Away!"

16
The Trial

Rebecca's trial was to take place in Templestowe's great hall. The Grand Master, dressed in flowing white robes, sat at the front of the room. All the other Knights Templar were seated in rows below him. At the far end of the room, a large crowd of peasants from the neighboring village crowded in to watch the trial, for news of the exciting event had spread quickly outside Templestowe's walls. The mood was so quiet and serious that not a sound could be heard in the crowded hall.

At last, Rebecca was led into the room. She wore a veil over her face and walked with her head down and her arms folded, looking at no one. Suddenly, someone thrust a scroll of paper at her. She took the paper into her hand but did not read it.

As Rebecca reached her seat before the Grand Master, she glanced around the crowded room at last, searching for a friendly face. But there was none.

The Grand Master looked around, and his eye caught Sir Brian. The knight was not seated with the others but instead stood alone in a corner of the room. One hand held his cloak up to hide his face, while the other hand traced patterns on the floor with the tip of his sword. "See how this trial upsets him," the Grand Master whispered to one of his companions. "He cannot even look upon the face of the woman who has bewitched him!"

As soon as Rebecca was seated, the trial began. Witness after witness stepped forward from the crowd to speak of Rebecca's effect on Sir Brian. Then a poor Saxon peasant was dragged forward to speak of Rebecca's amazing healing skills. "Two years ago," the peasant said reluctantly, "I was working for Isaac of York, when I fell ill. I could not move my arms and legs. I could not even get out of bed. This woman, Rebecca, came to my side and spread a spicy-smelling ointment over my limbs. After that, I could walk and move again. I cannot think that the woman meant me any harm," he added, looking over at Rebecca shyly.

"Do you still have the ointment she gave you?" the Grand Master asked. The peasant nodded, and the Grand Master demanded to see it.

Two doctors were present at the trial, and the Grand Master asked them to examine the ointment. The doctors said that they had never seen such materials and that Rebecca clearly had created an unholy potion. **Because Rebecca can do something the doctors cannot, they assume she is evil. Unfortunately, people didn't understand much about science and medicine during the Middle Ages. In fact, the so-called "doctors" of the day were actually barbers or animal surgeons, not people who went to medical school. So it's not surprising that someone who has studied the natural power of herbs could do a better job of healing than the "real" doctors could.**

"What do you have to say to these charges?" the Grand Master asked Rebecca. "Remove your veil and stand before us."

"The women of my people do not uncover their faces when alone in a roomful of strangers," Rebecca said.

Rebecca's voice was sweet and soft, and her polite dignity impressed many of the people gathered in the hall. But the Grand Master refused to let Rebecca's grace soften his heart. "Remove her veil!" he ordered his guards.

Two of the knights stepped forward to do as he commanded. "Wait," Rebecca said, turning to face the Grand Master. "For the love of your sisters and mothers, do not treat me so roughly. It is not right for a maiden to be handled by strangers. I will do as you ask." So saying, she removed her veil. Her beauty caused whispers of surprise and admiration all around the room.

When she spoke again, Rebecca's voice was full of emotion. "I know asking for your pity and understanding is useless. Nevertheless, I will say that I have always done my best to heal the sick, no matter what their religion. I cannot help it if my methods are different from yours. All I can do to defend myself is call upon Sir Brian. Speak, if you are truly a man, and tell this company whether the charges against me are true or false!"

Sir Brian looked up. His face flushed, and his lips moved without making any sound. Finally, he managed to say, "The scroll, Rebecca! The scroll!"

Rebecca glanced down at the scrap of paper that had been handed to her as she entered the room. Written on it were the words "Demand a champion!"

"Rebecca, clearly this knight will not speak for you. He talks in riddles," the Grand Master said. "Have you nothing else to say?"

"I deny the charge and maintain my innocence," Rebecca said in a strong, clear voice. "I demand a trial by combat and a champion to defend me." With that, she stripped off one of her gloves and threw it on the floor. **Throwing down a glove in front of an enemy was an official way to show you wanted to fight him. Trials by combat were common in the Middle Ages. Each side would pick a champion, and the champions would fight. If an accused's champion won, he or she was declared innocent. If the champion lost, the verdict was guilty.**

"Who would be willing to take up a challenge on behalf of a Jewish sorceress?" the Grand Master asked doubtfully.

"God will provide a champion," Rebecca said firmly. "There must be someone in merry England who will risk his life for honor and justice."

Rebecca's courage and dignity affected even the Grand Master. He gazed at the beautiful woman before him, alone, friendless, yet defending herself with so much spirit and courage. "Confess your witchcraft and renounce your Jewish faith," he said to her, "and I promise all will go well with you. What has your faith done for you that you should die for it?"

"It was the faith of my fathers," Rebecca said proudly, "and I will die for it if that is God's will. Please allow me to call for a champion."

"Bring me the glove," the Grand Master demanded. He rubbed the delicate material between his fingers. "This is indeed a slight and frail symbol for such a deadly purpose," he said. "See, Rebecca, how light and thin this glove is compared to one of our heavy steel gauntlets? So too is your cause against the Templars' faith."

"Add my innocence to the scale," Rebecca said, "and my glove of silk shall weigh more than your glove of iron."

"So be it," the Grand Master finally agreed. "Who will fight for the Templars?"

"Let Sir Brian be our champion," replied one of the knights. "He knows the truth of this matter."

The Grand Master agreed. At Rebecca's request, a messenger was sent to Isaac of York, asking him to find a champion to fight for his daughter's life in three days' time. Then the trial was adjourned.

As twilight fell over the castle walls, Rebecca was saying her evening prayers in her room. She heard a quiet knock at her door. "Enter," she called, and Sir Brian stepped into the room.

Rebecca drew back at the sight of the man who had caused her so much suffering. "You have no reason to fear me, Rebecca," Sir Brian told her.

"I do not fear you," Rebecca answered proudly, although her heart was beating quickly. "But you are no friend. Because you dragged me here against my will, I am facing a horrible death. What more do you want of me?"

"I never imagined things would turn out this way," Sir Brian admitted. "My future is also at risk, for my reputation as a Knight Templar is ruined. But there is one way in which I can save both my reputation and your life. England is not the whole world, Rebecca. Run away with me, and we shall find a place where I can find new paths to greatness and honor."

"That can never be," Rebecca answered. "I could never love a man who breaks solemn vows for his own selfish pleasure. You seek only what is good for you, and you care for no one else."

"You are proud, Rebecca, but so am I. When I face your champion in the lists, nothing will stop me from doing my best and fighting with all of my strength. And if I defeat your champion, you are condemned to die a horrible death. Let me take you away from here! It is the only way of saving your life."

"I am not afraid of death. I tell you, I would rather die than do as you ask!" Rebecca said with such confidence that Sir Brian knew she would never change her mind. "Please, leave me now. I have nothing else to say to you."

"Is this how we must part?" Sir Brian said quietly. "If this is how it must be, I wish that we had never met! Farewell, Rebecca," he said sorrowfully and left the room.

Sir Brian has not only put Rebecca in terrible danger with his selfishness but also caused trouble for himself. Either he loses his reputation as a knight—something more important to him than just about anything else—or he causes Rebecca's death.

17
King Richard Returns

It's been a while since we've seen our friend Ivanhoe. Where has he been all this time? You might remember that his friend the Black Knight rescued him from the burning castle and took him to a religious community where he could recover from the wound he had suffered at Ashby. The plan was for Ivanhoe to meet the Black Knight at Coningsburgh as soon as he was well enough to travel. Meanwhile, the Black Knight and Wamba head off for Coningsburgh and Athelstane's funeral.

Wamba and the Black Knight rode through the forest, joking and singing. "I wish that our friends Locksley and Friar Tuck could be with us as we travel through the greenwood," the Black Knight said.

"So they could be, if you would summon them with the horn that hangs from your belt," Wamba replied. "At least that horn will allow us to pass through these woods in peace."

The Black Knight patted the horn, which Locksley had given him to summon help in case of trouble. "What do you mean?" he asked his companion. "Do you think Locksley's men would attack us if we didn't carry this pledge of Locksley's friendship?"

"I say no such thing," Wamba replied quickly, "for these trees may have ears. But tell me this, Sir Knight. When is an empty purse better than a full one?"

"An empty purse is never better than a full one," the Black Knight said.

"You don't deserve a full purse if you believe that!" Wamba said. "Having an empty purse is best when you travel in the greenwood."

The Black Knight chuckled, and the two rode on. After a time, Wamba said, "I think the time has come for you to show what a powerful fighter you are. I see a group of men ahead in the trees, and I think they are lying in wait for us."

"What makes you think so?" asked the Black Knight.

"Because they are not riding on the path, as honest men would do," Wamba replied.

"I think you are right," the Black Knight said. "Here, take this for safekeeping," he added, passing Locksley's horn to Wamba, who hung the instrument around his neck. Then the Black Knight closed the visor on his helmet just in time. Three arrows flew out of the trees and clattered against his armor.

"Come, Wamba, let the battle be joined!" the knight shouted, as a group of soldiers burst onto the path and headed straight for them. So great was his strength and courage that it looked like the Black Knight would win, despite the greater number of men facing him. But then the leader of the soldiers, a knight wearing blue armor, plunged a lance into the Black Knight's horse, killing it and sending the Black Knight tumbling to the ground.

Wamba blew a blast on the horn hanging around his neck, then rushed forward to help his friend as best he could, for he carried no weapon. Just when it seemed the enemy would have the victory, Locksley, Friar Tuck, and the rest of the outlaw band burst out of the trees and lent their strength to the Black Knight. Soon all the enemy soldiers lay dead or wounded, and the battle was over.

"I wish to see these enemies who attack me for no reason," the Black Knight said. "Wamba, open the visor of the Blue Knight's helmet."

Wamba did as he was told. To the Black Knight's surprise, the face under the helmet belonged to Waldemar Fitzurse. "Who sent you on this traitorous deed?" the Black Knight demanded of the injured man.

"Your brother," Waldemar said, recognizing the Black Knight as King Richard.

Richard's eyes sparkled with anger, but he forced himself to be calm. "I want you to leave England and never return," he told Fitzurse. "If I hear that you are in this country, I swear I will hunt you down and kill you. Locksley," he said, turning to the leader of the outlaws, "bring me one of the horses that survived the battle and see that Fitzurse leaves us without injury."

"I would rather send an arrow after the villain and save him the trouble of a long journey," Locksley muttered.

"You must do what I ask of you," said the Black Knight, "for I am Richard of England!"

At those words, spoken in a tone of great majesty, all the outlaws knelt before the King to give him reverence.

They swore their allegiance and begged his forgiveness for any crimes they might have committed.

"Rise, my friends," Richard said, smiling. "Any crimes have been forgiven thanks to the loyal service you showed before the walls of Torquilstone and the help you have given me this day. As for you, Locksley—"

"Call me Locksley, no longer," said the leader of the outlaws. "I am Robin Hood of Sherwood Forest."

I knew it!

"King of outlaws and prince of good fellows!" Richard exclaimed. "Word of your brave deeds reached me even in the Holy Land. Be assured that I have forgiven you also."

The King saw that Friar Tuck was still on his knees. He walked over to the Friar and asked, "What is troubling you, my friend?"

"My dear King, you have been to my home and have seen that I don't live the life of a poor hermit," said Friar Tuck.

The King laughed. "I thought the deer meat in your pie tasted familiar. But don't trouble yourself over stealing a few of my deer. You are forgiven."

At that moment, Ivanhoe and Gurth rode into the clearing. Ivanhoe's impatience had driven him out of his sickbed, and he was now headed for Coningsburgh with the loyal Gurth.

Ivanhoe was shocked to see that his friend the Black Knight was really King Richard. "Why do you worry the hearts of your faithful servants and risk your life by traveling and fighting alone?" he asked. "You are the King of England. You would think your life had no more value than that of a simple soldier!"

"I desire no more fame than my sword can bring me," Richard said. "I am prouder of my solitary adventures than I would be if I led 100,000 men into battle. Now, let us have some supper and resume our journey to Coningsburgh for Athelstane's funeral."

King Richard sounds like my kind of hero!

18
A Ghostly Visitor

When the King, accompanied by Ivanhoe, Wamba, and Gurth, arrived at Coningsburgh, he found the Saxon castle crowded with people. A huge black banner hung from the top of the tower, announcing that the castle was in mourning for the dead Athelstane, and everyone who had known him had come to pay their respects. Gurth and Wamba soon found some friends in the courtyard, while Richard and Ivanhoe made their way into the castle in search of Cedric.

Cedric was staying in a large room on the third floor of the castle, which could be reached only by climbing a long flight of stairs. That climb gave Ivanhoe plenty of time to cover his face with his cloak, for King Richard had told him it was important that he not reveal himself to his father until the proper time.

Cedric was seated in the midst of a number of important Saxon lords, but he rose when his friend the Black Knight entered the room. **Remember, Cedric doesn't know yet that the Black Knight is really King Richard.** Cedric led Richard and Ivanhoe into a small side chapel where the body of Athelstane lay. The two men said a brief prayer over the body, then went into another room to talk.

"Do you remember when we last met, you promised

to do me a favor in return for my help in rescuing you from Torquilstone?" Richard asked. Cedric nodded. "Up to now, you have known me as the Black Knight. Know me now as Richard, King of England!"

Cedric stepped back in complete astonishment. "You are a Norman, yet you have proven yourself to be a man of justice and bravery," he said in wonder, recalling all the Black Knight's marvelous deeds.

"And now for my favor. I ask you to forgive your son, Wilfred of Ivanhoe, and restore him to his rightful inheritance."

Cedric looked at Richard's companion and recognized his son. "Wilfred!" he cried.

"Father, please grant me your forgiveness," Ivanhoe said humbly.

"You have it, my son," said Cedric, clasping his hands. Ivanhoe started to say something, but Cedric would not let him. "I know you are about to speak of the Lady Rowena, whom you love. She was to wed Athelstane, who is now dead. She cannot even consider another marriage until a suitable period of mourning passes. To do so would be such a dishonor to Athelstane, his ghost would rise from the dead and stand here before us!"

It seemed as if Cedric's words had indeed raised a ghost. Scarcely had the words left his lips when the door flew open and Athelstane himself stood before them, as pale as a man just risen from the dead!

Cedric leaped back and leaned against the wall as if he would fall without its support, while Ivanhoe and Richard began to pray. "If you are a ghost, tell us why you are here, so we can set your spirit at rest," Cedric demanded nervously.

"I am not a ghost," Athelstane said calmly. "I am alive—or as alive as any man can be, after what I have been through! It's terrible—I haven't eaten for three days!"

"But I myself saw you struck down by Sir Brian at Torquilstone and thought you dead," said King Richard.

"You thought wrong. I was not killed by the Templar's blow, only stunned. For the past days I have lain senseless, but now I am whole again."

"What a wonderful day!" Cedric cried. "Here is a Saxon noble worthy to rule England. Tell this Norman prince, Richard the Lion-Hearted, that you will challenge him for the throne of England."

"What?" Athelstane cried in surprise. "Is this the noble King Richard? I give him my allegiance, heart and hand."

Cedric was stunned. "But think of the future of the Saxons in England," he begged his friend.

Athelstane shook his head. "Being near death has given me wisdom. If I were to challenge King Richard for the throne, war and the death of thousands of innocent folk would result. No, I will not do it."

"What about Rowena?" Cedric demanded. "Do you intend to abandon her too?"

"Cedric, my friend, be reasonable," Athelstane said. "Rowena loves the little finger of your son's glove more than she cares for my whole body. Here she stands to swear to that," he added, for at that very moment Rowena hurried into the room. "Give me your hand,

Rowena," Athelstane said. "I will give it to my friend Wilfred and announce that I renounce my claim to you. Wilfred?" he said questioningly, looking around the room. "Where has he gone?" For the place where the knight had stood was empty.

Everyone was stunned at Ivanhoe's abrupt disappearance. Rowena could not hide her disappointment. How could her beloved Ivanhoe leave so quickly? They finally had a chance to be reunited. Where could he have gone? The servants were questioned, and finally Cedric learned that a Jewish man had slipped into the castle to talk with Ivanhoe. He must have carried urgent news, for no sooner had Ivanhoe heard what the man had to say than he called for Gurth and his armor and hurried away.

I'll bet the messenger came from Isaac! Rebecca is in desperate trouble, and Isaac has asked Ivanhoe to help her. Ivanhoe is Rebecca's only hope. Can he save her life?

19
Trial by Combat

The day for Rebecca's trial by combat had arrived. The lists at Templestowe were packed with people, as if every surrounding village had poured forth its residents upon the scene.

The Grand Master sat on a throne at one end of the lists, underneath a banner decorated with the symbol of the Knights Templar. Near him sat Sir Brian in his battle armor, his face pale and drawn, as if he had not slept for several nights.

Rebecca was led in by several guards and taken to a black chair at the other end of the lists. Beside her, a pile of branches had been arranged around a tall wooden stake. Rebecca would be burned to death should her champion fail to save her. When Rebecca saw the stake, the reality of what she faced made her shudder and close her eyes for a moment. Then she turned her face away.

"Here is Sir Brian de Bois-Guilbert," the Grand Master proclaimed, "ready to do battle for the Knights Templar against the champion of the witch Rebecca." He then turned to Rebecca and said, "No champion has appeared to fight for you. Do you expect anyone to come and battle for your cause, or do you yield yourself to your doom?"

"I maintain my innocence," Rebecca said firmly.

"The day is not yet finished. God will provide for me in good time."

"We will wait until the sun is in the west to see whether a champion appears," the Grand Master stated.

Everyone settled down to wait. After a time, Sir Brian made his way to Rebecca's chair. "Hear me, Rebecca," he whispered. "We can still escape. Mount behind me on my warhorse, and we will ride far from here. Let the Knights Templar erase my name from their records. I will go on to better adventures elsewhere, with you at my side! See, I am willing to give up everything I have, just to claim you as my own. If you do not come with me, I will die of a broken heart!"

"Go away!" Rebecca said. "Nothing can change my mind. I will face death bravely rather than do what you ask."

Hours passed. It seemed clear that no one would appear to defend Rebecca. But just as the Grand Master was ready to announce that they would wait no longer, a knight appeared on the horizon. As he galloped toward the lists, a hundred voices in the crowd shouted, "A champion! A champion!"

Rebecca's champion was a sad figure. His horse had galloped at top speed for many miles and looked about ready to fall down with exhaustion. The knight swayed in the saddle and seemed deathly tired and weak.

"I am a good knight who is ready to pledge my sword to this damsel, Rebecca," he said. "I say the sentence pronounced on her is a lie, and I will defend that claim with my life!"

"What is your name?" the Grand Master demanded.

"Wilfred of Ivanhoe," said the knight, raising his helmet so all could see his face.

"I will not fight you now," said Sir Brian. "You have recently suffered a serious wound, and your horse is done in. Once your wounds have healed and you have a better horse, I may agree to fight you."

"Have you forgotten that you have fallen beneath my lance twice before?" Ivanhoe asked scornfully. "Have you forgotten the vow you swore at Rotherwood to fight me once I returned to England? I will proclaim you a coward throughout the land if you do not do battle with me now."

Sir Brian flushed with anger. "Take up your lance then, and prepare for the death you have brought on yourself!"

"Rebecca, do you accept this man as your champion?" the Grand Master asked.

"I do," she said softly. The sight of Ivanhoe come to save her, affected Rebecca even more strongly than the fear of death had. "But wait," she added. "Your wound from the tournament at Ashby is still fresh. Why should you fight and die now?"

Ivanhoe's only answer was to lower his visor and pick up his lance. Then he and Sir Brian took their places at opposite ends of the lists. The Grand Master signaled that the battle should be joined, and the knights headed toward each other at a full gallop.

Ivanhoe and his exhausted horse were no match for Sir Brian's strong charge, and both horse and rider fell to the ground from the force of Sir Brian's lance. But to everyone's surprise, Sir Brian also swayed in his

saddle and fell, although Ivanhoe's lance had barely touched him.

Ivanhoe quickly rolled out from under his fallen horse. He drew his sword, ready to face Sir Brian, but the other knight did not get to his feet. Ivanhoe stood with one foot on Sir Brian's chest and pointed the tip of his sword at his throat. "Yield to me or die!" he demanded. Sir Brian did not answer.

"Do not kill him!" the Grand Master shouted. "We declare him defeated. You have won the challenge."

The Grand Master hurried to Sir Brian's side and pulled off his helmet. Sir Brian's eyes were fixed and glazed, and his face bore the pallor of death. Untouched by Ivanhoe's lance, he appeared to have died of a broken heart, torn apart by the violence of his own emotions.

"This is indeed the judgment of God," the Grand Master said.

When the shock and surprise had passed, Ivanhoe asked, "Have I done my duty as Rebecca's champion?"

"You have," the Grand Master replied. "I pronounce the maiden innocent of all charges." He turned to Rebecca. "You are free to go."

Just then, a company of soldiers thundered into the lists. At their head was the Black Knight. He turned around and pushed up his visor to reveal his face. "Know that I am Richard, King of England!" he proclaimed. "This land is once more under my rule."

Rebecca saw and heard nothing of King Richard's triumphant return. She was locked in the arms of her father, who had stepped forward from King Richard's riders and rushed to her side.

"My darling daughter, my recovered treasure," Isaac said, "we must thank the man who has saved you."

Rebecca glanced quickly at Ivanhoe. "No," she said. "Oh, no. I dare not speak to him at this moment. I might say more than I should. No, Father, let us flee from this evil place."

"You cannot leave without thanking him," Isaac said in surprise.

"I cannot speak to him now!" Rebecca cried, her voice shaking. "For my sake, Father, we must go!"

Isaac reluctantly agreed, and the two fled the field as fast as they could.

20
Happily Ever After

Cedric the Saxon was a stubborn man, and he still dreamed that Rowena and Athelstane would marry. But Athelstane refused to go along, and it was clear that Rowena would marry no one but Ivanhoe. At last, Cedric gave his consent and allowed the wedding to take place.

The wedding of our hero and his lady was celebrated in the beautiful cathedral at York. **A cathedral is a huge church. The cathedral in York, called York Minster, is one of the most magnificent churches in all of England.** It was obvious to those that were in attendance, that Rowena's and Ivanhoe's joy knew no bounds. They were safe at last in each other's arms—their love was a lifelong commitment. King Richard himself attended, and the church was filled with both Saxons and Normans. Perhaps King Richard's influence helped temper the hatred the two groups had for each other.

Two mornings after her wedding, Rowena received word that a woman wanted to see her alone. Curious, Rowena agreed.

Her mysterious guest entered. She was a noble

figure, wearing a long white veil that only added to her elegance and dignity. The woman knelt at Rowena's feet and kissed the hem of her robe in a gesture of profound respect.

"What do you mean by this?" Rowena asked in surprise. "I am not a queen that you should honor me this way!"

The woman looked up, and Rowena recognized Rebecca. "To you, Lady of Ivanhoe, I pay the debt of gratitude I owe your husband for saving my life in the lists at Templestowe."

"Ivanhoe was merely repaying the debt he owed you for your care when he was wounded and imprisoned," Rowena said. "Can I do anything to show my thanks?"

"Nothing," said Rebecca, "unless you would give your husband my grateful farewell."

"Are you leaving England?"

"Yes," Rebecca said. "My father and I are going to Granada, where we have friends. **Granada is a part of Spain.** We do not feel safe in England."

"Surely you have nothing to fear," Rowena said. "You have Ivanhoe's protection. There is no reason you cannot stay with us. I will be like a sister to you."

"That cannot be," Rebecca said sadly. "A wide gulf separates us, and custom and religion make crossing it impossible for either of us. You are fair and good and beautiful, Lady Rowena. I bless God for uniting Ivanhoe with—" Rebecca could not finish. Her eyes overflowed with tears. "Forgive me," she said after a moment. "My heart fills when I think of what Ivanhoe and I shared at Torquilstone and Templestowe. Farewell, my good lady."

She glided from the room, leaving Rowena surprised and thoughtful. Later, she told her husband of Rebecca's visit, and the story made a deep impression on him. He and Rowena lived happily together, for they loved each other very much. But Ivanhoe could not help thinking, from time to time, of Rebecca's beauty and courage.

Ivanhoe distinguished himself in King Richard's service and rose high in his favor. Life was filled with everything Ivanhoe valued—fame, adventure, and the love of his dear Rowena.

What a great book! It has everything a good story should—daring deeds, romance, the mystery of men in disguise, and plenty of adventure. All this excitement has made this little dog sleepy! And there is nothing better after a good adventure than a good nap!